# Child Witness

## Renee Ritchie

*A silent traumatised child holds the clue to a callous crime.*
*Who will solve her secret?*

Paperback ISBN: 978-1-7638133-0-4
Ebook ISBN: 978-1-7638133-1-1

First edition
First published 2025
Author photo by
Cover design by Graham Davidson
Typesetting by Rack & Rune Publishing

Published by Renee Ritchie

# Prologue

Tess started fitfully, surfacing again from the inner darkness which kept clawing at her, pulling her under. In the space surrounding her, she could dimly make out the moon submerged behind a cloud bank. Rather than helping her adjust to the gloom, the seeping lunar light created a fine mist in her eyes, which only served to conjure more ominous shadows around her. She shuddered amidst the cold vapour rising from the damp, raw earth.

Tess tried to brush loose the hair stuck to her brow and felt blood trickle down the inside of her neck. It was oddly comforting in the chill. She felt overwhelmed beneath the dark sky, that was indifferent to her injuries. Yet the cool breeze helped to rouse her, connecting her to her situation – but she still couldn't understand.

*What am I doing here?*

She concentrated all her effort into remembering. Pain shot up the back of her neck. The thumping in her temple intensified like someone had thrown a volume switch, except only static filled her ears.

In a blur she recalled the *thump* of her head on the windscreen…a vague *crunch* of boots on gravel and glass…the yellow slipper strewn in the ditch. Realisation hurtled through the fog of her mind.

*Rachel! Where was Rachel?* A silent scream that couldn't escape her parched throat.

*Crack.*

*Was that a twig breaking?* There it was again. The unmistakable sound of someone or something moving steadily through the bush.

She shrugged deep down into her woollen turtle-neck pullover and bent her face to her knees, as if assuming the crash position.

Tess's breathing quickened; heartbeat roaring, she imagined that the sound filling her head could be heard outside of her body. The wound on her head oozed sickly. She tried to piece together what had happened but could only grasp at fragments. Finally, groggily, she got to her feet, trying to decide if the sound meant help or harm; but she lost her footing, staggered and fell backwards. The ground disappeared behind her and for a long-partial second she felt weightless, before plummeting into an abyss of unconsciousness, yet again.

Unaware of the drama it had created, a stray cow shuffled and nosed around the scrub.

# Part 1

# The Kids

"Quick! I hear a car coming. Head for the tunnels!" The two sun-bronzed girls broke free and dived to either side of the unsealed road, disappearing into the protection of the child-high grass that flanked the lane. They gripped fistfuls of loose gravel, as if unwilling to surrender ill-gotten gain.

No fluorescent orange council worker had ever been sighted on these country roads. The slashing of grass was left to the locals, who in turn left it until they got around to it, which was hardly ever.

Through the anonymity of the straw-coloured walls of their hidden roadside tunnels, the children watched the cloud of dust get closer until a battered white utility materialised, like a mirage wobbling in the stinging noon-day sun. They rained a scattering of stones from their childish fists onto the vehicle as it passed. Few made an impact. Nonetheless, the sound of stones sprinkling over the car bonnet, delighted these cherubic criminals. On hearing the engine slow and splutter, the pair launched off in different directions to escape detection. Each child propelled themselves through the carefully flattened tunnels. Creating their own catacombs occupied many of their waking hours and they'd succeeded in adding an impressive stretch of chambers. Playing and hiding along the road was even more fun than playing in their beloved cubby houses.

Rachel began to tire first, her heart thumping, her chest bursting as the adrenaline rush faltered. The wiry eight-year-old stopped abruptly and flopped down on her back like a felled ghost-gum, singing *timberrrrr!* Arms and legs spread out, she looked up at the unbroken sky, but quickly closed her eyes against the glare. She smiled. So very still was the day and she too lay motionless for what seemed like a long time to her, but it was likely only moments, as she imagined herself to be part of the landscape. An echo of The Dreaming.

She breathed in the dry smell of her chamber and tuned into the crackle of the brittle grass as it swayed in the breeze. Peering through the red of her closed eyelids, she was mesmerised by the shapes which danced before her in silhouette. She may have slept a moment, who knows? Yet soon enough, the scratchy grass digging into her bare neck, roused her. She slowly moved her arms and legs to make the bush equivalent of 'snow angels' in the long grass, extending her secret chamber. She squinted, making castles in the sky above.

She heard Anna calling her name. It was a good idea to make noise now. Mum had taught her that it was important to make vibrations with your feet and voice, to give the snakes an opportunity to slink away. Rising, she rejoined ranks with her best friend so they could plot their next reconnaissance mission.

As they scuffed along the road, there was only one other occasion that the girls needed to hide from an approaching car. They thought better of scattering any more stones on car bonnets. Instead, the new challenge they set themselves was to avoid being seen by anyone, whether on the road or paddocks either side of them, as they made their way back to 'base.' Any sight or sound of their neighbours saw them dive inside the tunnels of waving grass. They arrived back at Rachel's home thirsty, but in great spirits. Grabbing water and their bikes, they pedalled to the hills.

The Budginigi hills were an easy fifteen-minute pedal, for children always so brimful of energy. As they cycled, squinting into the sun, the first one to spy the rocky outcrop let out an ecstatic whoop. Yellow box, red-gum and stringy bark stood in small stands around the base of Budginigi, so it was not difficult to find some shade to park their dragsters under. They drained the rest of their water in one gulp. The girls had examined the base of the steep rocky mound many times - there were always new paths to safely wind their way up. Big and Little Budginigi lies between Tabletop and Ettamogah on the purported Hume and Hovell Track. The oldest farmers in the district believed that the two explorers never climbed either rise, but merely noted the hills in their early diaries and maps. Not so for Rachel and Anna. Each time they found a new way to conquer the summit gave them a buzz.

The girls navigated the most obvious track. There was so much they wanted to cram into their day of freedom. It was quite a short distance up even the bigger rise, but slow going because of steepness in parts. This meant the little girls had to clamber up and over rocks; it only added to the experience for them. But they didn't enjoy sharing the narrow track with the cattle, which were allowed to graze on the crown land.

After sweating and panting, they finally reached the top and were rewarded with a 360-degree panorama. The vista incorporated views of Table Top Mountain to the East, whilst the extensive Hume Weir snaked far and wide around the scene. The remnants of the original mob who owned the land, would murmur that these hills were women's sites and should not be climbed at all. The children were oblivious to this, but did share a sense that the place was special. Rachel and Anna could never sum up their attachment to the location. It was simply their place. In the earnest imagination of small children, they accepted as fact, *their* ownership of the land they played on. This included the run of the hills and the rest of their neighbourhood. They were intrepid explorers. They embraced it all: the slopes, the dry paddocks, the flattened corridors alongside the road, and the pine trees at school. All of it belonged to them.

Anna, leading the expedition back down the hill, got a kick by holding back the stretchy branches of tender saplings that crowded the track, then letting them go at just the right moment to hit her companion fair across her raised arms, intuitively lifted to protect her face.

Thunk.

The two were equals in that blissful state of childhood, full of protests of laughter, rather than cries of outrage or pain. Country kids were a rollicking, adventurous lot.

Of course, there is always an exception to every rule...like the time when Anna tumbled over the handlebars of her speeding bike and belly flopped down the long dusty incline of Mitchell Road. She was a mangled, bleeding mess. Quick-thinking Rachel raced back home to get help, the yellow ribbons on her dragster handlebars flapping frantically in the wind. Rachel was torn about leaving her friend's side. She'd been busy comforting Anna, shooing away the incessant flies that worried at the wounds, attracted to the stickiness and smell of skun flesh. Then she realised she'd have to get a grown-up to bring a car to retrieve and untangle her poor, sobbing friend from her bike.

For days afterwards, Rachel watched, fascinated as Anna's mother tended her daughter's wounds. Patiently, she painted copious amounts of Betadine over the raw skin and picked out tiny stones as they worked their way to the surface of Anna's grazed stomach. Rachel was wide-eyed and respectful, and in outright awe when the gravel rash began to scab. Anna said her tummy would *crunch* as she began to slowly move about. Of course, Rachel was relieved too, when her friend's intense pain finally gave way to mild discomfort.

"Kids bounce back quicker than grown-ups," the neighbourhood parents would always say. Lord knows they had ample opportunity to test the truth of this homily.

# the **Policeman**

## 1

The town's only cop pulled into the school yard and waited for the bell. Even though Table Top Central School boasted only twelve robust students, they were sourced from just five families. His daughter Anna was an only child, but her preferred playmate, Rachel, was both mischievous and likeable – like her Mum. Whenever the officer eased into the school in his marked car, Rachel's mother, Tess Moloney, would make a feeble effort to fumble with her seatbelt as she spotted the law drive in, then shoot him a quick half-wave. Rachel in the back was always safely strapped-in, but Tess just never got into the habit of fastening her own seatbelt on the country roads. One of the many attractions for Albury folk who decided to move to this outlying tiny postcode, was the laid-back lifestyle.

It had all become something of a predictable morning and afternoon ritual as the young mother swept into school in her drab-blue Corolla, the driver window open, spilling snatches of song from *The Little River Band,* and spent ash from her cigarette. On cue, Tess would bestow her winning smile on the officer in apology for her laxness.

Today was no different to any other day. Sarge grinned at Rachel as she tumbled out of the Corolla, glancing over her shoulder at him and smiling, waiting for Anna to catch-up. A tight pack of school children waited ready to sweep them off into some merriment in those precious moments prior to the clang of the school bell. Sarge's own beribboned daughter exited the car, eyes already fixed on her friends and the fun ahead of her, though not before giving her dad a kiss with mock reluctance and pulling his police cap down over his eyes with affection.

Sarge noted Tess's departure from the school yard with a touch too much acceleration than the occasion required. He deliberately didn't look to see if her seatbelt was properly fitted. He did note the determined approach of the school groundsman, so he made his escape and headed into the station, before he could be embroiled in a long chat or complaint. He pulled out of the yard slowly, allowing the dust Tess's driving had created a chance to clear.

'Sarge' as he was named, was cool. He could have made trouble for Tess about more than not being buckled up, if he'd wanted to. It was the early seventies in small town Australia; Tess did not fit the paradigm of a country mum. Whilst Sarge was brisk, he was also kind and didn't sweat the small stuff. Plus, Tess Moloney was ridiculously young and a pretty good looker, which might have helped just a little. He chose to ignore the gossip and innuendo which followed her. His wife, who didn't usually gossip about locals, had sized up Tess as one to be pitied, envied and begrudgingly appreciated. Quite the cocktail. One Saturday afternoon when they bumped into Tess at the General Store, the missus remarked wistfully to Sarge that Tess was completely unaware of how her natural prettiness and animated conversation, drew glances of admiration of the men (and women) around her, wherever she went. Sarge knew that his wife Sarah, would have been aghast at being perpetually ogled, and certainly wasn't coveting attention. He had squeezed his wife's hand and caught her eye. She had intelligent and beautiful eyes that he could lose himself in— so deep in fact, that he thought at times he could be drowning in the blue depths. Sarah was complicated. He was less so. He knew that Sarah was out of his league, yet this quiet, classy girl who he'd been taking out to dinner every weekend, had said *yes* to his marriage proposal. Truthfully, marriage had not changed his feeling that Sarah was still just out of his reach.

Maybe his basic decency made him a better catch than he gave himself credit for. Sarge had been a sharp police recruit for sure and had advanced beyond the rank of Constable speedily. Yet these days, he had no ambition beyond his current role and status. Becoming a family man made it easy for him to turn his back on endless days of overworking to climb the so-called ladder of success. He was content to be Station Sergeant at Table Top. He had settled into the easy lifestyle of the hamlet, after a normal adjustment period. He and his wife weighed up the limitations of a tiny rural school for their only daughter, against the wonderful sense of community. His missus had been educated at a large establishment for girls in a stately Melbourne suburb, but she had felt awkward and invisible. Fair to say, Sarah had colluded with this dynamic by successfully shrinking herself in any social scenario because of her natural shyness. Sarah didn't want that for her daughter, however. This small, friendly school in the country was highly desirable in the minds of both Sarge and his wife. No fear of their precious Anna not being seen or known at Table Top Central. Without siblings, or the likelihood of more to come, the students were like family, especially Rachel.

2

Banging the front door of the station, Sarge called out, "Any messages, Nancy?"

Nancy was mostly only in the office on Tuesdays and Thursdays and was very hit-and-miss with even routine administrative tasks. Looking down her nose through the glasses perched precariously on the end of her nose, she relayed,

"Just one, boss. An anonymous complaint about a suspicious male hanging around the school when the kids were playing… on the forest side… the caller didn't want to get involved but thought you should know, Sarge."

"Who on earth would be watching? The school is hardly rush-hour at Pitt Street," Sarge quipped.

"A lot of holidaymakers from Victoria have been camping at the weir for the speedboat races, so maybe some weirdo is hanging around with that lot, and was doing some wandering? You know that Melbourne taskforce just busted up a big paedophilia ring," offered Nancy.

"I saw it on the news."

*Bless Nancy,* resounded in Sarge's thoughts.

She had a heart the size of a barn, but possessed an unmistakable parochialism, mixed with her easy country hospitality. Sarge had to admit he often encountered this, in the little village which was now his home. Often, any source of trouble was due to a local on a bender, to escape the pressures of farming; or a kid relieving the boredom of the sleepy circadian rhythms of Table Top. Yet it was typical of Nancy, and many in the town, to reckon that an outsider was responsible.

Nancy was naturally kind and fair-minded, even if small-minded, yet the scope of her world was not extensive. She was the daughter of a fourth-generation farmer and had never strayed far from home. She was no snob, just a great lover of her community, and generous to a fault with its people.

Sarge liked her belief in those around her. In his job it was a welcome antidote for him to experience optimism and an assumption of decency in others. Nancy's gracious outlook in life, lent her to search for an imported problem or perpetrator, rather than betray her loyalty to the people of her beloved town. Many of Sarge's policing mates who had stayed on in city-units for their whole careers, were cynical and jaded about human nature.

Nancy was a lovely soul, whose local knowledge and care for their township served him well as he manned the Table Top Station, otherwise solo.

"Did you want to look at the phone report after a cuppa? I brought you in a jam roll to have, it's still warm from the oven," she wheedled. Not that Sarge needed a lot of convincing.

The portly policeman sat down on the office chair. He sighed contentedly, munching on the spongy treat, licking the sugar dusting carefully off his fingers. That diet his wife had been nagging him about certainly didn't apply to Nancy's baking days. It would have been rude to knock back such hospitality and not practical to dent the pride of the reigning president of the Country Women's Association. With one last swill, he drained the scalding black tea, and with a frown of concentration gave his full attention to the typed phone report in front of him.

Whilst Nancy had provided a generous morning tea, the details she supplied in her phone report were scant. A suspicious medium-height, medium-built man with fair, flowing long hair, had been sighted that Thursday parked near the school yard, smoking and watching the kids play at recess.

No precise time. Nothing about the make of the car, and of course, no number plate had been given. No name or number to call back.

The policeman sat back in his chair thoughtfully.

*Suspicious,* he suspected in this case, could well mean *different* or *modern.* Most of the farmers around here still favoured a short back and sides, even though it was beginning to be fashionable for men to have longer hair in the city. It might be common in Melbourne but was viewed with suspicion here in Table Top. At best, long hair in a bloke marked him as an outsider here. At worst, it was assumed he was anti-authoritarian, probably a hippie, or even a drug dealer. Sarge sat back in his chair. At the pub on the weekend, one of the old guys commanding the bar, said that he had it on good authority that

Tess Moloney's ex was sniffing around. Talk was that the hurried teenage wedding in Sydney had only yielded a short-lived marriage. It had ended when Rachel Moloney was a toddler, with Tess driving her useless husband to the train station and bidding him goodbye from her life. A bold move for a young mum, but one which turned out to be street-smart. Sad that the little girl didn't have a dad around, but Tess and Rachel were likely better off without a drifter who didn't provide for his family and had only half-heartedly applied himself to dabbling in petty crime.

*S'pose I shouldn't be too scathing in my assessment of 'im,* owned Sarge.

Rumour had it, Moloney's husband's own upbringing had been tough and that he himself was barely a man when fatherhood had surprised him.

"Fathering kids is the easy part, raising them is another matter," grumbled Sarge to no one in particular.

Nancy looked up from across the room and then went back to her crossword puzzle.

Hopefully he could get it right with his own daughter, he reflected. Big responsibility, but it brought more fulfilment than he'd ever imagined. He reckoned it could well be James Moloney wanting to catch sight of his offspring, but not bothered enough to show himself, in case God forbid, that meant he would be required to help or contribute to the bills for the kid's upkeep.

Nancy parachuted into his thoughts. "Hey boss, what's a seven-letter word for blood relationship?"

Sarge replied, "Kinship."

## the **Mum**

When Tess was on the cusp of childhood and adulthood, she had dreamed of moving to the city and trying floristry in Melbourne as a career. Maybe she could even learn to drive? She had brimmed with excitement when thinking of the freedom and opportunity a driver's licence would bring. Of course, that was before her life had veered sharply off an unexpected exit-ramp.

As a little girl, Tess had toyed with the idea of being a teacher, inspired by the *Anne of Green Gables* stories. Prior to consuming Montgomery's series of books however, eleven-year-old Tess had even sincerely considered being a nun. Perhaps many girls from Catholic schools entertained such romantic notions, without really being aware of what such a vocation entailed. In Grade Six, Tess, along with most of the other girls in her class, took the veil of Holy Communion and committed to loving memory the catechism with wide-eyed devotion. Certainly, inspired notions of service and sacrifice found fertile ground in Tess.

Well, that was all before a sour, red-faced Sister at her high school punished Tess by battering her hand with a ruler, for what was only a minor act of rebellion. This marked the turning-point where Tess began to truant and not turn in her homework on the occasions when she did make it to school. In one fell swoop, any dreams of studying education or taking Holy Orders, were crushed. Funny how things work out. The influence of teaching nuns should have ticked all the boxes for Tess as a high school student. Not so.

A strained school experience, combined with an awkward, strict father, who struggled with knowing how to handle losing his pet-child to the strange effects of puberty, set Tess Moloney on a collision course.

Tess would still shudder when recalling the shouting match that came when she refused to come downstairs to go to Mass with her family, one infamous Saturday evening. She was suffering from the inconvenient arrival of the monthly curse-cramps and bleeding, which had rudely interrupted other plans, such as her swim-training that week, as well as church. Suffering both pain and embarrassment, she had resorted to lying miserably on her bed.

Ordinarily she didn't mind going to Mass. She found a quiet comfort in the rituals and hymns at her local parish church and had instinctively wanted to share its magic with others. One winter's morning, after a slumber party, she had taken a friend with her to Sacred Heart's morning service. Tess vividly remembered the intense effort of stifling fits of giggles, as her guest was completely bewildered by the ever-changing standing, kneeling, crossing and chanting deal. This, combined with the bitter cold rising from under the pews and the disapproval emanating from the congregation, meant Tess would never again invite other girlfriends to share her beloved rituals.

Tess had loved the smell of the creaking wood pews and trace of sweet incense in the air. She revelled in the sun glinting through coloured glass, enlivening the Bible stories captured there; a holy hush around her. As an impressionable child, Tess had genuinely personalised and cherished the times of singing favourite hymns, such as, "Abide with me" and "Amazing Grace," in her pure soprano. As she approached her teenage years however, she realised that some of the rituals, and especially the austerity and unfriendliness of her church environment, were at odds with the sweet simplicity of the Gospel message that she'd cherished from a young age.

Now in her memory, the peal of the church bell heralding *Evensong*, morphed with the of the belt her Father was removing, as he pounded up the stairs, ready to mete out corporal punishment. A terrible moment of panic had ensued. Far from buckling under, Tess ran off like a startled bird.

Nothing was ever the same again. Another line of demarcation. On one side was her child-self, immersed in a home life she loved dearly. On the other side was her teen-self: a runaway, a rebel.

At fifteen years of age, Tess fled to a girlfriend's house where she spent an uncomfortable night sharing a hard single bed. The next day convinced that she couldn't return home, Tess hitchhiked to Melbourne. She was accompanied by the girl's older brother who'd assured her that he'd find her a place to stay with a distant relative in a big, draughty old house. Supposedly, this was safe enough, but there were other boarders there, and she soon found that there were strings attached to this living arrangement.

Tess became just another country kid fleeing to the bright lights, finding only compromise and coercion, packaged as survival.

What a blur! Doctor's appointments. Shocked silence at the other end of the phone. A rushed wedding. Her father scowled at their invited guests; multicultural Melbourne proving way too much for him to adjust to, he frequently retreated to catch the score of the football grand-final, which dominated the wedding day.

Tess was a radiant bride in her pink, fashionable mini-dress and tasteful white hat. Her gloved hands, trimmed perfectly with pink ribbon, laid protectively across her middle. A child bride, hopeful for the future. Youthful naivety persisted even amid this crazy redirecting of her life.

# the **Kids**

## 1

Sunday. Glorious Sunday. Another whole day stretched tantalisingly ahead of little Rachel Moloney. Mum had long abandoned any ruse of going to church on this, the Lord's Day. Rachel munched on cornflakes and Vegemite on toast, dripping with butter. Faithfully, she made her bed (to Tess's exacting standard), tidied her room and packed away her completed jigsaws. She fed the chooks and collected the eggs. When finally released from chores and the confines of the house and yard, Rachel met up with Anna who was waiting, scuffling in the front drive. Together they plotted their first adventure of the day.

Tess overheard "Let's pretend," as the kids huddled, hatched and tested the viability of each potential scheme. Having settled on a game plan for the morning, Rachel and Anna set off before Tess thought of any additional chores for them. They whooped gleefully across the front yard, side-stepping the moving balls of white fluff, otherwise known as Chinese Silkies. It was obvious to the locals that the Moloney family were really townies as there were few regular chickens scratching around the yard, but instead, plenty of exotic poultry underfoot. The two girls kept well away from the red-gold Bantam rooster as it savagely pecked a discarded football, as though it was its rival.

The kids took turns pretending to be crows, competing and jostling, never agreeing on who called *caw caw* the loudest. What a sight! – flapping their arms and jogging wildly down the dirt road.

As they approached the end of the lane, the main object of the day came into view, demanding that they cease their noisy carry-on. Foster's Farm. Anna and Rachel suddenly became solemn, though they shared a glint in the eye as they occasionally nudged each other. As deftly as they'd avoided their mothers' strict instructions to keep their adventures away from neighbouring properties, they skirted the perimeter, patiently locating the spot they'd been hunting for. Here they could trespass undetected, or so they hoped.

Mind you, the kids probably would have been invited to look at their chosen object, if they had presented themselves at the front door of their neighbour's cottage and asked politely. Where would be the fun be in that, though? They preferred instead to sneak around, spying out the farm, pretending that ol' Foster was the enemy and they the heroes of the day.

"You go first Anna! I'll hold the wire up for you…that's it. Watch your head…come on don't sook," coaxed Rachel.

"It's not as easy as it looks!" said Anna.

Rachel helped push her friend through a convenient gap provided by the ditch beneath the barbed wire. Then it was Anna's turn to help Rachel through, carefully holding up the wire, avoiding the sharp sections.

They hugged, giddy with getting into the property with only minor scratches and scraped knees. They could hear Fred Foster swearing near the side veranda as he grappled with some tools and machinery, even though he was a long way off. The girls covered the distance from the fence to the shed quickly and quietly. Creeping with seriousness and intent that mimicked the most dedicated guerrilla, they peeked through the teeny gaps in the wooden slats of the shed. They were equally as good at making a racket, as operating with stealth and silence.

"Beaut," hissed Rachel, "we can go in, the coast is clear!"

The kids carefully approached the stalls, crooning soft, reassuring sounds to the patient ewes, as they visited the first of the lambs. Lambing season was magical. They would have loved to touch the soft pure white of the mewling lambs, but the pair took particular care to only appreciate and not touch the newborns. Even as kids new to farm life, they understood that they should never touch newborn lambs in case this confused the scent for the exhausted ewes and resulted in them rejecting their own offspring. This had been painstakingly explained to the fascinated Rachel when she'd become the proud carer of her own pet Lambsie, when her mother had rejected her.

Nature's design is that ewes are attracted to amniotic fluid for a few hours after birth, which stimulates nuzzling, sniffing and licking behaviour. After a relatively short time the mothers become familiar with the lamb's unique odour. Thereafter, lambs without odour or with other smells introduced, are almost always rejected. Of course, after some time, the ewes learn to use visual and auditory cues to identify their lambs, and smell becomes less important than it is at the beginning.

The girls were a captive audience, safely screened, for a long time. They crept out of their hiding spot to look for other newborns, then slunk towards the opposite building, rounding the side of the woolshed, and there they stopped in their tracks. Their idyl was broken, their senses assaulted. The donkey tied to the post, in the next stall, aimed one final kick at the lifeless mounds of what was once softness and cuteness – now a mess, streaked with blood. Oh dear! These were the twin lambs the children had excitedly heard had also been born. The news of their safe arrival had motivated them to make this mission in the first place. The twin lambs had been quarantined in supposedly the safest place. It seemed barely possible that the brute of a donkey could have been bothered, let alone been able, to reach the vulnerable creatures. The donkey now stood deceptive and docile. The two girls, however, could not un-see the brutality they had witnessed.

Anna began to cry. The magnificent spell the glorious day had cast was shattered like the shards of a favourite Christmas bauble. The eagerness and excitement cruelly evaporated. Rachel herself had a lump in her throat. She'd made the twenty kilometre move from Albury to the tiny village of Table Top the year before but wasn't yet insulated from the harshness of farm life.

"Let's go!" they said in unison.


## 2


They quickly put as much distance between them and the crime scene, as their little legs could manage.

After a rest under a tree and with the resilience of children, they were not quite ready to go home. Stealthily they skirted some back paddocks, imagining that they were out of eye-line, in case Rachel's Mum was looking their way as she worked in the back garden. Rachel led the way to the other side of the property into the area she well knew was out of bounds. The dam was in her sights.

Once when a male caller for her mother was visiting, Rachel had been allowed to spend an afternoon with Tess and the hopeful boyfriend at the normally forbidden dam. It was hilarious fun as she slipped and slid along the edges, helping to bring in the crayfish pots, which housed the captured red-orange yabbies. Squealing, Rachel eye-balled the pincers, from a safe distance. The crustaceans made a delicious meal later with lemon and homemade salty chips. It had been a memorable day, as would be expected of any day when a child is permitted to embark on a normally outlawed activity, which ended in a delicious treat.

In the first week that Rachel had moved to the house in the middle of the dry paddocks, she'd been sat down and told sternly that she was never ever allowed to go to the dam by herself. Even when Rachel did her chores, and released the ducks from the prison of their pen in the mornings and watched them waddle towards the dam, she knew not to go any further.

So even though she felt a pang of guilt as she approached the dam now, Rachel reasoned that she wasn't alone, even though she knew full well that a grown-up, not another kid, was meant to accompany her.

As they approached the waterway, Rachel repeated gleefully and with great ceremony the tale of the Bunyip to Anna (who lived on a house block). Most Australian farm dams are not fenced off and to avoid drownings, a hair-raising mythology is told to wide-eyed kids – of an enormous, slimy, bulging-eyed monster lurking in the muddy waters of the lagoons and dams in the interior of Australia, waiting for naughty children to devour. Not only was Santa Claus earnestly believed in, but the existence of a Bunyip in each of the dams on Burma Road as well. True, Rachel had doubts, but she could never discount the possibility entirely.

The well-meaning folklore was reinforced at the Ettamogah Sanctuary a few kilometres down the highway, which boasted a motorised Bunyip experience, a favourite outing for Tess to take Rachel on. The Sanctuary also housed a wonderful koala enclosure where families could walk the wooden platform and see the cuddly Aussie mascots interacting lazily in their own habitat. There were many bird aviaries to visit, ponds teeming with water birds, a dingo enclosure and a home for a ringtail possum. Once, when she was lucky (and quiet) she'd been privileged to spot an echidna as it shuffled across the yard. Always a reluctant *Prima Donna*. Walking through the grounds, heady with the scent of Eucalypts, there were kangaroos and wallabies to watch around the twenty-five-hectare park.

Rachel's mum had learned the hard way, not to linger at the fence of the emu paddock. Many a tourist had been caught out, mid-Polaroid, with the long-necked bird coming way too close for comfort, frightening them as it sidled up to pose for the camera. Emus make the most disconcerting low, thumping grunts which can be heard two kilometres away. At close range, it made the local kids laugh hysterically to see the reaction of an unsuspecting city visitor.

The highlight of the day, that made heavy legs lighter, was the promise of the final exhibit near the exit. For a spare twenty cent coin, Rachel and Tess gained access into a viewing room and woke a horrible Bunyip. Even before the ears of the grotesquely comic creature rose from the water, it scared the mother and daughter with its sudden booming roar.

Yet, despite this unsettling threat, Rachel Moloney led Anna defiantly all the way to the prohibited dam. Wisely, they were wary of the slippery sides of the reservoir, but once there, Rachel and Anna seemed unsure of what to do. It had been thrilling to approach the site undetected, but now with the sun high and their heads unprotected by a hat or the shade of a tree, they were unenthused. They remembered that their stomachs were empty, and their throats parched. They tried to skip stones across the receding muddy water without a lot of success, giving up when they realised that the sticky mud on their sneakers would betray them.

They scampered away from the dam and back to the tap at the side of Rachel's shed. They hosed the tell-tale mud from their shoes and jeans; - but then they had the problem of having to explain why they were so wet. Rachel couldn't think of an excuse that would keep her out of trouble, so she just lurked about the yard waiting to dry. Anna pedalled home, and with her mother in the kitchen, she slipped up the stairs and changed into some fresh clothes, shoving the offending items under her bed until later.

Poor Rachel had to resort to gulping water from the hose and sunning herself on the far side of the shed as she waited to dry off; meanwhile Anna tucked into a lovely, cooked meal, which her Mum always provided when Sarge could make it back home on his lunch hour. Rachel, ever innovative, thought to scrounge for some old apples stored in the shed. Strangely, when she tried the door handle it was locked. It never had been before. She tried to peep through a grimy window, gingerly avoiding the spider webs. She rubbed her eyes a few times, adjusting to the low light and stream of dust mites. Scratching her head, she stared perplexed at what she saw crammed into the dusty space. She threw herself back down and leaned against the shed. Tilting her head to the sun she closed her eyes. It could've appeared a peaceful scene to an onlooker, if not for the slight frown on Rachel's face as the little girl automatically twisted tendrils of her already windblown hair, deep in thought. Later that night, and with the assistance of large handfuls of hair conditioner, Tess had painstakingly brushed out Rachel's sun-bleached hair, which was intricately knotted on one side.

# Sarge

Sarge was reopening the station after his lunch hour, when with a groan he sighted Bob's car pulling up in the driveway. He'd hoped to finish off mounds of paperwork, and then return home to spend the last hours before dark poking around his veggie garden. It was a glorious day.

He instantly regretted his decision to evade the school groundsman-come town-gossip and gripe, earlier that week. Now he was trapped without an escape route. No Nancy to cover for him – she never worked on a weekend.

"Sarge… these bleedin' kids!" spluttered Bob as he took off his hat and leaned on the front counter. The policeman had not for even a moment thought that this was just to be a neighbourly chat. One look at the old man as he came into the station revealed that Bob was fit to burst with whatever was bothering him.

"I swear mischief is never far away with that lot. Anna and Rachel have been seen roaming the countryside, and I reckon I know who the ringleader is. Come to think of it, they're always out-of-bounds at school too. I can't prove it, but I reckon Rachel's buggered up my ride-on. It's totally stuffed and won't start. I found the petrol cap removed and a water bottle nearby. I reckon it's *Tess's* mongrel kid that did it! For some unknown reason the brat has put water in my mower tank… but she left behind a blonde hair! Who in the school has hair whiter than little Rachel Moloney?!"

The groundsman raised his voice and eyebrows simultaneously, with what was irrefutable evidence in his mind.

"It's uncalled for vandalism, I'm gonna give the mother a piece of my mind," he spat out.

"Bob, Bob!' Sarge interrupted calmly, "I'd go easy before you say any of that to Mrs Moloney."

"*Mrs* Moloney, I think not!" Bob snorted. "Tess ain't got no ring on her finger and is pretty much a child herself raising a child! If that's what you could call her sort of parenting. Look, her kid is nice enough I reckon, and seems real smart, but she has way too much freedom – which you would do well to consider, because she is inseparable from your daughter."

Sarge opened his mouth to respond, but was left looking like a gaping goldfish, as Bob ranted, hardly drawing breath. "That's not all of it. The word is that Tess's music is loud enough that the next property could join the party on their own porch – and there ain't any town blocks on Burma Road, you know what I mean? Geez… not to mention the types you see riding out to her place on their Harley's on weekends."

*Liking a party isn't no crime on its own*, the policeman reflected, as Bob went on and on with his monologue.

Sarge had been a regular country lad through and through, playing footy and drinking with his mates. He'd certainly been to his share of parties when escaping the discipline of training at the Goulburn Police Academy. He smiled to himself, recalling the wild celebration, (well, what he could remember of it) at the after party, when he and a few mates had gone to the Collingwood versus Carlton VFL grand final in Melbourne. Cheering with the record crowd – the atmosphere was electric. He and his mates hadn't slept that night, singing and drinking euphorically 'til dawn. Of course, he felt rough all day after. Nowadays, he reckoned that moderation was better.

Rousing himself from his reverie, he thought it time to take charge of the conversation if he was going to enjoy any of his Saturday afternoon.

"Seems to me Bob, that with Tess relocating here from Albury, she's made a good move, especially if she was prone to find trouble there. Mate, how about you give a young mum a break? Is there an official complaint you wanna bring?"

"*Young,* I'll say! No argument there Sarge. Mildred from the post office says that she was sixteen when she had her baby." On and on Bob grumbled and gossiped. Sarge relented, recognising he couldn't turn back the tide. He allowed the one-sided conversation to crash and fall in waves over him, adding the occasional grunt or nod at appropriate intervals. Letting Bob get it all out of his system was all that was really required from him. He knew the old guy didn't want anything other than someone to listen to him yarn. It was really a barter system. Sarge exchanged patience and a listening ear, and in return, Bob gave the policeman peace and quiet for a spell. The old guy was lonely. His wife had passed, his daughter taken too early by cancer, and his only grandson had grieved his way into rebellion and trouble with the law. Most people made allowances for Bob's crusty manner on account of this. Sarge knew professionally that it was better to scratch an itch, instead of withholding the thing he could give so easily to remedy a situation. Human nature can be so stingy when meting out sympathy, agreement or encouragement.

Sarge, listening with only one ear, pursued his own musings. He liked Tess and Anna saw a lot of Rachel, so Bob's tirade provoked him to feel a bit protective. It couldn't be easy being the target of talk from an entire community, even when Table Top only boasted a population of one hundred and fifty or so. In fact, this only made Tess more conspicuous and vulnerable. Truthfully, he felt more empathy for the Moloney family than he could muster for Bob's complaint. Not that he would let his Anna spend too much time over at Tess and Rachel's home; things there might be a bit more *laissez-faire* than he and his missus' preferred for his Anna. Tess herself seemed to possess some good instincts when it came to raising Rachel. It was just the crowd who hung around the young woman that he didn't trust. Well, maybe, he admitted to himself, the Moloney's were not the most functional family unit. Humans are wonderful beings, yet complex, fragile and flawed. Surely though, every family, including his own, had a level of dysfunction. *Some more than others.* His work with teenagers from troubled contexts, with coaching young boxers at PCYC, showed him that kids have trust issues.

Sarge roused himself.

"*Orright, Orright, Orright* Bob. I'll have a chat with the little tacker and Tess, when, or if, I reckon it will do some good. Can you just give it a rest now, please?"

Bob nodded curtly. "Come round home for a beer when you're driving past, Sarge," he muttered. Himself, or one of his antecedents, had lived on the corner near the railway crossing for generations. The ramshackle collection of outbuildings trailing the cottage did not mean that the homestead was without charm. The yard and garden were lovingly maintained. Bob was always welcoming, finding time and swapping stories with locals who swung by on any one of the three verandas that wrapped around the cottage.

"Righto, when I'm off duty of course."

"Course," Bob responded with a wink.

"Catch you soon then mate! I must finish up here so I can get home to Sarah and Anna. I'll call by next week."

# Tess

1

The new week was not going to plan for Tess. School days meant that she could get a few things done without the responsibility of watching out for Rachel. She'd also been looking forward to a date of sorts – a guy she'd been seeing here and there had arranged to pick her up for a windswept ride, and then lunch together at the pub. She knew that she shouldn't be quite so bitterly disappointed, but sometimes she still felt like a restless teenager – even at the age of twenty-five.

She grumbled to herself all morning as she tried to set the house straight.

*If it's not one thing, it's another!*

*May as well work as a hospital orderly!*

*Motherhood is pretty much cleaning and bedpans… Thank goodness nappies and toilet training are done, though. Still, it's really shift work, without pay… and no days off!*

Tuesday's topic of self-conversation was Tess moaning that Rachel was home sick from school. Afflicted with mumps-again! Once was enough, but to contract mumps twice, a year apart, was unreasonable and excessive, to even the most optimistic and experienced parent. Mumps in the house was also a deterrent for male company.

Tess's daughter had already acquired a swag of common childhood illnesses. When added to the endless scrapes and bumps, Tess considered herself quite adept in distracting her sick or injured child. She was doing her utmost to care for Rachel today, even in her disappointment.

2

Tess intuited that her child was a wondrous gift to her. Even before Rachel was born, she'd brushed off any hint that her child would be disadvantaged because of her own youth. For a while, Tess consumed any reading material she could lay her hands on about birth and parenting. With a dedication she hadn't found in high school, or in other parts of her life, she tackled tomes of research. She tried to grasp content from complicated journals from the State Library. Enjoying the tram ride to Melbourne city library, she settled into this reading ritual in the long days before she gave birth. She loved the quiet cool which enveloped her once she walked through the impressive front doors. It was so welcome after the closeness of her dingy flat with its watery grey walls, and lingering smell of old milk – no matter how hard she scrubbed every surface. Tess loved the smell of the books. Situated at Shakespeare Place, the library appealed to her sense of romance. It was a sensory and aesthetic pleasure.

In the end though, she halted her vociferous reading about early-childhood development, when her routine changed with the move to Sydney. Her husband found higher-paying work in a Redfern factory. Tess had to admit, too, that she was getting stressed by all the information she was digesting. There were too many frightening statistics to absorb. Premature birth or complications were a real risk for her, because of her young age, or so she'd read. When she voiced her concerns to her family doctor on a visit home, he had kindly patted her on the hand, reassuring her that while motherhood so early was not ideal, she was healthy, and her own mother had delivered six children safely.

Rachel was born premature as predicted, but birthing her six weeks early was still frightening, even though she'd prepared herself for this contingency. She never wanted to experience that worry again. Her baby was ridiculously tiny, weighing less than three pounds. Tess held her breath until that magical moment when she finally heard Rachel's first gasp for air. Oh, how she welcomed that sudden, strident life-affirming wail.

Rachel remained in intensive care for months at The Royal Women and Children's Hospital in Paddington. Not that the teeny baby needed ventilation for long, but she failed to thrive while cocooned in the sterile safety of her humidicrib. Free from germs, but sadly, separated from cuddles too. Strict hospital rules of the day discouraged human touch; ironically, just what is required for premature babies to gain weight. Tess tried to visit her baby regularly after she was released from hospital. It was a mammoth effort. A two-hour long bus trip, and she was only permitted to look at her baby girl, covered in wires and tubes in her glass box. Then the long, emotional trip home. It all proved unmanageable. Tess felt redundant. It made more sense to her to pick up some shifts at the nearby corner store, until she could finally hold her baby in her arms.

Emotional, as would be expected for a new mother without her baby, and lonely, in a volatile marriage of convenience, her impossible situation came to a head on day twenty of motherhood. Tess had fretfully stirred at first light after an interrupted slumber on an especially steamy Sydney night. There'd been shouting on the street below and loud music. Tess would always be able to recall the scent of frangipani, heavy in that close, airless room. She'd turned towards the bassinet next to her bed, positioned in readiness for Rachel's release from hospital, with her eyes only half-open. With horror she comprehended the steady progress of a cockroach, the size of her hand, over the pristine white cotton sheet, trimmed with pink satin.

Tears of outrage streaming down her face, Tess rallied to action. She snatched up her things from that grimy, loveless place that was never her home, and called a taxi. Fighting through morning traffic, the taxi arrived at Central Station with the narrowest of margins for Tess to make the mail train, which eventually deposited her wearily at Albury station.

Later, when her husband got from home from night shift, he'd found an empty flat, a note on the dresser, and the smashed carcass of the offensive pest on the bedroom floor, a potent picture of their shell of a marriage.

It took three excruciating months for Rachel to reach the requisite five pounds in weight, for her to be permitted to leave the special care nursery. It was truly a wondrous day when Tess was at last allowed to bring Rachel home from the Sydney hospital. Her family willingly provided the funds for a return air-ticket to Albury, in the collective excitement of meeting the baby.

Tess kept the Polaroid that forever memorialised this coming-home event, propped up next to her jewellery box with her other humble treasures. It showed a radiant girl in a pale green suit, complete with stockings and crème pumps, standing on the tarmac with an aircraft in the background. Looking proudly into the camera, Tess cradled her treasure, wrapped in a soft white blanket.

The months living with her family were amazing. With love and without complaint, Tess's mum assisted with the punishing regimen of feeding Rachel every two and a half hours throughout the night. In the day, there was always a younger or older sibling on hand, to help hold or distract Rachel when she fussed. There were many to share the milestone moments too. Her own father had softened a little and begrudgingly snapped Polaroids of Tess sunning baby-Rachel in the gardens. There were photos of Rachel sitting up and playing with toys in an enormous playpen on the front lawn.

This oasis evaporated all too quickly when Tess moved into a spartan flat when her husband rejoined them – a second chance to build a family. Her father made it clear that it was time for Tess to leave her family home and make her own life. Mum and Tess's sisters still helped her when asked, but they had their own lives, and it was not like the previous live-in help.

Tess really was on her own. Her husband was more of a liability than an asset. The marriage soon ended, before husband and wife had a chance to mature on their own, let alone together. Rachel was barely two years old when Tess severed the bogus partnership, driving Rachel's father to the train station. That was that. Instantaneous relief. Tess in fact, had one less person to manage, from that point on. Financially, the difference was negligible. The supposed breadwinner of the household often spent his Friday pay-packet at the pub – shouting round after round of drinks to newfound friends, leaving Tess distraught at how she was going to make rent. He went back to Melbourne. She battled on alone trying to live up to the demands of adulthood. The divorce was speedy, with ample evidence of infidelity on his behalf, expediting proceedings. Tess drew a line under this era with finality, demonstrated by taking the extraordinary step of not seeking financial support from him. He was unreliable and his family uninterested. She got out of Sydney. Tess shrugged off Rachel's dad's lineage like a tattered outer garment which had never fitted her life comfortably.

Yet within the drama compressed into Tess's young life, and the stigma attached to young divorcees, she encountered real moments of enjoyment as she struggled to be a family to her child. Rachel was not developmentally impacted by her rough start in life. She was brighter than most of her peers and very advanced in her reading. It was expedient, but also a source of maternal pride that her daughter had gone to school at four and able to read. Sending Rachel to school so early wasn't just a knee-jerk reaction to having a kid so young and wanting to get on with her own dreams and plans, but it was the fashion of the seventies to start children on their educational journey at the tender age of four. Tess knew beyond doubt that her daughter was school-ready. *A mother can judge best* she reasoned, when pangs of guilt or loss threatened to overwhelm her.

Even as a harried young mum, Tess had read book after book to her child. It had calmed them both. Wrapped in stories, they had relaxed and bonded together – eating up some of those endless lonely hours which hung heavy in the house.

Tess knew that she made a lot of mistakes as a mum, but she worked hard, mostly solo, to foster camaraderie between the two of them. She'd painstakingly educated family and friends to not treat them as oddities, just because they weren't a text-book family. Tess was fiercely protective of her child. Her problem was working out how to handle the row of men that she seemed to attract.

Sadly, while Tess had succeeded (mostly), in protecting her child from harm, she could not say the same of herself. She oscillated between allowing dubious men into her life, to sabotaging relationships which may have worked. As captivating as Tess could be, having a daughter who already had the number one place in her heart, did not help her find a long-term mate to share her life with.

3

Tess reminded herself again of how much she adored Rachel. She breathed deeply, the sweet country air, grateful for this fresh start with her daughter in Table Top, surrounded by a little bit of land and animals. She was always tripping over a wandering feathered or furry ally. Ordinarily she didn't do well with chaos, but somehow life at Table Top was different. Tess didn't always have the same sense of being overwhelmed and lost. In fact, she didn't mind feeling out of control when those feelings were generated by such an adorable menagerie.

She sent Rachel on a small errand in the house that she felt the little girl could cope with on her wobbly legs. Mercifully, the fever was staying down. Tess looked out indulgently as their pet lamb came over to the glass doorway, which was all that separated outside from inside. Rachel giggled and pulled faces, pressing her lips against the glass and leaving a sticky mess from the remnants of food in her mouth. Tess had only cleaned the glass the day before! She was about to lash out with words that had sprung up as if from a poisonous well, deep inside her …

*Dirty girl…*

…but stopped herself, in time, shocked that she'd been about to fling this bomb at her sickly only child. In the past she hadn't always succeeded in stemming a bitterness that spewed forth terrible things. On several occasions she was mortified that a previous love interest had stepped in between her and her child to build a wall against incoming nastiness.

She struggled with her shame, but forced herself back to the present, helping Rachel to manoeuvre the huge sliding door open, as the patient coaxed Lambsie to come into the family room. Both wobbled on their legs, Rachel doubling over in laughter at the sight of the lamb's slapstick-skating, with hooves not made for the polished tiles. *Lambsie* was confused at the best of times, having been hand-reared by Tess and Rachel and shut in with the ducks upon nightfall. The weakened lamb had been rejected by the ewe who'd birthed her, but now Lambsie pulled on her milk, stronger each day. The pet lamb provided quite the entertainment. She'd follow the waddle of ducks down to the dam in the day, even going in as deep as her knees, before halting. Then she'd linger, bleating at the ducks gliding away from her, before making her way back to the yard. Of course, Tess thought that

Rachel had only witnessed this funny sight on the couple of occasions when Tess herself had been across at the dam with her. Like many parents in the country, with unfenced waterways on their properties, she'd sat her offspring down solemnly and pledged her to never go to the dam without a grown-up. Tess had deliberately perpetuated the belief that a bunyip lived in the water.

Tess sincerely hoped (and yes even breathed prayers) that her good instincts would make all the difference needed. She just knew that she'd made the right decision in her move to this tiny village. It was a lovely lifestyle, and she was grateful for her family's help to secure the rental. She'd have never been given the property to lease if her father hadn't used his influence. She left behind a party scene which had been pulling her away from this vocation of motherhood. She sighed. It was hard being so young and having so many responsibilities. Sometimes she felt fit to burst with the conflicting desires within her. At times she craved freedom, almost as if it was a palpable thing - like a caffeine fix which forced its way into her bloodstream.

Despite this, she had done what she knew to do. While she struggled to find the time to play with her child once she was out of babyhood, reading to her had been more of a natural fit. Tess had expended much time and love immersing Rachel in stories and words. An investment in her imagination. Would this weave a better story than could be told from her other impulses or lapses of judgement?

Tess sighed as she tidied the kitchen and returned an array of condiments to the pantry shelf. It seemed like half the morning had disappeared trying to coax Rachel to take the medicine required to bring her fever down. She had attempted to mix crushed paracetamol with peanut butter, and then jam, but it didn't seem to disguise the taste. Rachel only brought it back up mechanically in a foul mess. Finally, Tess had cut the tablet in quarters and cunningly placed each inside spoonful of chocolate ice-cream. Success! Rachel was terrible at ingesting tablets. It seemed physically impossible for her to swallow any pills. Perhaps it was more of a mind problem, the tired mum mused to herself. Her little girl had begun her life with tubes thrust down her throat.

*The days were long and the years short.* It was a cliche for good reason. Tess determinedly walked past the liquor cupboard above the fridge. Eyes ahead, not daring to even look at it.

*Much too early,* she chided herself.

# Rachel

## 1

This was the first time that Rachel had needed to be kept home sick for some time. The last drama was an injury as opposed to an illness. Rachel had run shrieking up the backyard last November, with her new playful Kelpie pup nipping at the frayed hem of her jeans. Their house at Table Top was incomplete (probably why they had been able to afford to live there) and was still without a rear porch. Broken bits of building detritus were scattered around the dwelling. There was a deep drop, from the laundry door to the ground. When Rachel had jumped up onto the slab to escape the dog, she'd collided with Tess who was coming out simultaneously to see what the cause of the commotion was. Rachel had just turned to see if Benji was still at her heels, toppled over and fell headfirst off the ledge. Three stitches meant that Rachel had a visible scar on her previously unmarred forehead.

Tess marvelled at Rachel's strange mix of resilience and vulnerability. Terrified of a gorgeous puppy, playfully biting her with admittedly needle-sharp teeth, yet she'd scarcely flinched when with eyes dry, she was stitched up at the local clinic. It was only when the injured child was told she had to miss school, that her eyes had become moist. Rachel had perked up when she was deposited onto the couch in the sunken lounge room, with the plush orange shag carpet. This was normally out of bounds for the grubby girl when she came in from playing.

The incident resulted in the puppy dog, going away and then mysteriously never coming back. The Moloney menagerie still included a pet lamb, various breeds of exotic chooks, and ducks- Muscovy and Pekin breeds. All this for a little family which never had so much as cared for a goldfish previously. Rachel and Tess embraced life on their small hobby farm.

"Mumps! Again…not fair," Rachel grumbled to her Mum and out loud to the creatures around her. However, she took solace in the treat of her lamb being permitted inside with her. She laid her head wearily on the lamb's flank, breathing in the smell of lanolin and dust. She brightened again as she experimented with placing her teddy in a position so it could sit like a rider on Lambsie's back.

2

Rachel hated being forbidden to attend school. Hated being away from Anna and her buddies. Hated missing out on anything. In the little girl's mind, mumps was a robber. Today was Tuesday, her favourite day of the school week. Enrolment in a single teacher school meant that she and Anna constituted all of Year Three. Rachel would be missed. Normally she and Anna would start the day together in the reading corner. They were expected to look at the books silently and with minimal fidgeting. Mr Holden would start the Upper Primary on their morning drills, casting a severe and penetrating eye in their direction as needed. He succeeded in cowering any culprit who did not remain completely silent.

Next, they'd be allowed to unpack the Cuisenaire rods and talk softly. They used the wooden blocks to help them with their basic arithmetic exercises. If they completed their sums correctly, they'd be rewarded with permission to use the varying lengths of rods to build imposing, coloured towers. The best part was when the time came to knock the towers down with great satisfaction, when the instruction of *pack-up time* reverberated around the school room.

At ten o'clock in the morning each Tuesday, the entire school would watch *BTN* on the rickety television set dragged out of the store closet by the school captain. Rachel loved watching *Behind the News*. She carefully formed her one sentence summary and drew a picture about each news item in her report book.

Lunchtimes saw the school disperse in their small year groups to the towering pine trees which enclosed the school perimeter. Each year grouping claimed a particular tree as their own territory. With nettles crunching underfoot, Rachel would run, embracing the fresh scent rising as the wind moved through the school yard. Such a welcome relief, an escape from the stifling summer heat of the classroom.

The whole school yard was circled by elderly conifers which formed a blurred boundary to the forest housing the same trees beyond the school on two sides of the wire fence. Rachel loved to collect up the fallen fir cones for their Christmas craft, or to put them aside for the fire bucket. She'd been captivated during the nature lesson by these beloved evergreens. They were an ancient and unique species which held almost magical properties for this fourth-grade child.

Rachel proudly and accurately related the lesson to her mother last week. She knew that conifers were not like other trees because technically they didn't have fruit or flowers. Instead, they developed their seeds in cones. Conifers tended to have male and female cones on the same tree. She remembered that the boy cones, which are smaller and more abundant, hold pollen which at different times is blown by the wind- a fine film, coating everything in its path. The girl cones, once fertilised with the pollen, bear the seeds. Amazingly, this process of producing pollen and seeds on the same tree happens at different times, to avoid self-pollination and guarantee genetic diversity. Rachel had struggled to get her head around all this information as the lesson was taught to all the children from Kindy to Grade Six, as was necessary at a one- teacher, central school. She loved how Mr Holden had used the firs in their playground to say how special every species on earth was and how much there was always so much to learn about nature. He had stopped before her table as he moved around the enthralled classroom with a male and female pinecone in each hand.

"I'm gonna miss the next nature lesson," moaned Rachel glumly to Lambsie, who gently nudged her hand. She wasn't the only one who was keen for the next instalment. Mr Holden was strict, but a masterful storyteller.

*"Tell us more, Sir!"* one enthralled sixth grader had called out, but not without raising his hand at the same time. Mr Holden could turn ferocious if class etiquette was ignored. On this occasion however, he overlooked the fact that a student had spoken out of turn. Grinning indulgently, Mr Holden had said,

"All of creation is fearfully and wonderfully made… we can't possibly cover it one nature lesson. Class dismissed!"

No further encouragement was needed! The whole school pelted en masse to the seating area, grouped around the giant pines. Chatting, they traded sandwiches and drinks from their bottles which had been frozen overnight and stashed in school bags, artfully wrapped in tea towels and rubber band to stop the moisture seeping into everything else. When the bell rang for the second half of lunch, the children were finally permitted to get up. They stowed their lunch boxes away, casting uneaten crusts to the waiting, friendly currawongs.

Rachel wistfully recalled how in that second half of lunch last week, the entire school, such as it was, had boisterously played British Bulldog 'til the bell sounded, signalling afternoon lessons were beginning. Anna had incurred a minor injury which briefly held up play, but remarkably even with the mad antics of big kids running at little children, there was a sense of fairness and decency which pervaded. The older ones were quite careful of the little ones, even if they teased them mercilessly.

Torturing herself with all that she was missing, Rachel lamented that she was stuck at home. Bored. Resentful.

*Mumps… again!*

# Tess & Rachel

"How about we go for a drive and drop the eggs off to Mrs Robinson's place? Would that cheer you up, Button? You'll get your pocket-money early, for helping collect the eggs last week." Tess used Rachel's baby name affectionately and fleetingly touched her daughter's nose. "No need to get dressed."

Still in her favourite pyjamas with pictures of cows jumping over the moon emblazoned all over them, Rachel scuffed along the driveway in her yellow slippers, swaying in a slow dance moving towards the car with Ellie, her stuffed elephant. She started to open the front passenger side door, her gloomy thoughts forgotten.

"Whoa there! I've already put the eggs on that seat Rachel, we aren't making scrambled eggs today! Hop in the back please."

Tess had already loaded the Corolla, gently nestling the delicate cartons into the towels laid out on the dusty seat, on the side closest to the creaking shed, where she stored her fresh produce. She gently led Rachel around to the back right passenger side and safely strapped her in. Not bothering with her own seat belt, she drove at a pace far more conservative than the young woman normally favoured.

"Mummmmm. Why so slow?"

"Precious cargo on board, Rach," she shot back, as she tossed the hair out of her eyes, quickly turning to wink at her. "Let's put some tunes on," she laughed over her shoulder.

*Tess had a laugh that could stop a war,* Rachel's Nan would often say.

Rachel loved having time with her mum when she was in a playful mood.

The radio cassette went in with a *click* and the sound of The Little River Band filled the car as they made their way slowly along the dusty road. They had surprisingly strong voices, for a frail child with a sore throat and a petite young woman:

> *With every day of my life*
> *I can surely see now where I am going*
> *And every day of this year*
> *I can clearly see I ain't wasted any time, no time at all*

They played air-guitar along with the solo, laughing playfully as the car slowly rattled along with eggs wobbling in the reused cartons. They turned right, off their road, onto Mitchell Road which would enable them to cut across to the farms close to the weir, on the other side of the range. After a moment of checking on both the eggs and Rachel, Tess paused at the intersection, then resumed the driving and her vocals:

> *Don't know why life's hard for us*
> *'Cause we sure do try*
> *Forget your cares and worries*
> *You know that we'll get by, yes, we'll get by*

The car crawled along the dusty stretch of road. Rachel grinned in the joy of the shared fun. Then her smile morphed into a grimace as she erupted into a coughing fit in the back seat. Tess cast a concerned look into the rear vision mirror, eyeing Rachel's wan and frail frame now convulsing with uncontrollable spasms. She bit her lip, second guessing if this little distraction she'd engineered, was such a good idea after all for her recovering patient.

It didn't take much for Tess to switch suddenly to self-doubt. Story of her life. Good moments easily drowned instantly in an incoming wave of guilt or regret. Reaching down next to her feet she retrieved her water bottle and tried to pass it over her shoulder to her gasping little girl.

Tess was completely unaware of the battered old ute as it flew up a narrow laneway, obscured by a line of poplars. The vehicle failed to give way at an unmarked T-intersection and slammed into the passenger side of the Moloney's car. The last thing Tess saw was a blur of white in her left peripheral vision. There was a sensation of unwittingly, in an instant, being flung forward. She heard breaking glass, and a surreal realisation that it was she who had broken that glass dawned on her, in a strange reel which seemed to happen in both one moment in time, yet also played out in horrible slow-motion.

# Rachel

Rachel blinked and picked off a piece of glass that had landed on Ellie the Elephant, glittering like a diamond tiara. Fortunately, she had instinctively closed her eyes when the car had been jolted and she heard the glass breaking.

The smaller than average eight-year-old struggled with her seat belt which had pinned her to her seat and would not release. Rachel persevered. She kept pushing the button in and wiggling the holder as best she could while being pressed so tight to the back of the seat. Eventually she won the battle and released herself from her confinement. She took a deep breath. On any other occasion she would have relished this small victory; it was a delight when she didn't need assistance from a grown up. This was not the occasion for childish pleasure or gloating, however.

"Mum, Mum?" She called out. There was no answer.

Rachel jumped from her door in a flash, but remained in the crouch she had landed in, next to the open door, shielded for a few moments longer from the horror of the scene. She gripped her comfort toy like her life depended on it, frozen in fear. Finally, she moved around the door. The child surveyed her mother who she could see crumpled, some metres away. Tess was motionless. Rachel thought she looked like an unwanted doll, fought over in a temper tantrum then discarded after the tussle.

Rachel was momentarily transported back to the time she and Anna had fought over a much-coveted hairdresser Barbie doll. Rachel remembered hurriedly demolishing the wrappings of most of her birthday packages but slowing down with the parcel from Anna, taking her time to carefully remove the green paper with sprigs of daisies on it, while Anna sat quietly, watchful and twitching. Eventually Anna interrupted Rachel's agonising delight by shouting out the contents of the gift on the top of her lungs, stealing Rachel's surprise, who uncharitably in return would not allow her best friend to play with the doll. This had not been the plan in Anna's mind after lovingly choosing the gift. Unusually for the pair, cross words had been spoken and Anna had slipped home. Before the day was out, Rachel had accidentally broken her cherished gift.

Rachel had not tired of again and again arranging her doll on the tiny swivel chair and pulling the hair dryer down over her head. She was most appreciative of the way the mechanism lit up and the timer went *ding* when Barbie's already perfect curls were set. The problem wasn't that she'd been rough with the doll, but rather that she'd grown curious about how it all worked and made the mistake of poking around in the wires at the back. Her disappointment in herself was acute, and she'd taken Hairdresser Barbie and flung her at the wall in a temper and overflow of tears. She'd stood red-faced and unnaturally still, as she appreciated with horror the doll lying awkwardly across some books in the corner of the bedroom.

Now Rachel was stuck in the grim present - unable to go forward for what seemed like an age but was only a moment. She was afraid to approach her mum. What if Tess was broken beyond repair? Rachel felt a pang of guilt grip her, the terror balling in the pit of her stomach. Was it her fault? She'd distracted her mum who'd been trying to help her as she coughed in the back seat.

All these fragmented impressions took only seconds to run through Rachel's troubled mind. Yet the childish abandonment to love unreservedly, trumped Rachel's fear.

*Wake up Mummy, wake up Mummy!*

The *crunch* of gravel and broken glass alerted the child. She was not alone. The other driver, who must have sat hurt or stunned at the wheel of his offending car for some minutes, had slowly summoned himself to action and was approaching the scene.

Rachel didn't look up right away, keeping her eyes on her motionless Mum. She saw the worn boots first. She lifted her eyes, shading them from the sun, now high in the sky.

"Shush…not a word to anyone about all this, little lady," the ominous voice commanded. The figure leaning over her was obscured for a few seconds by the dark spots dancing around the sunbeams in her eyes, like a crazy disco. The voice was familiar, like the singer of a song that she knew, but couldn't quite place.

"I mean it!" he snarled, "I can't go down for this, I just can't."

Rachel stood-up. Frozen, she observed him bend down, pausing the methodical wringing of his hands long enough to check the crumpled woman's pulse and slap her face half-heartedly.

"She's alive," he breathed softly. Yet it was equally evident to him, and to the child, that Tess wasn't moving at all.

"Bloody hell! Why didn't she wear her seat belt? Useless woman. This didn't have to happen," he raged to the chorus of magpies on the side of the road.

He stepped towards the child. She stepped back. His arm shot out and, placing a tight grip on her shoulder, he bent and whispered in her ear. Not the gentle assurances you might expect, but discordant words -short and sharp like a tune belted out in savage *staccato,* on her old piano at home. He took off his dripping cap and pushed back his coarse hair. Rachel thought curiously that she'd never seen someone sweat so much, like a tap suddenly turned on. He went back over to his car and started to rummage around in the back.

Rachel seized the moment, silently backing away the instant he turned his back. When his head was in the utility, as he cursed and searched for something in the back seat, Rachel turned on her heel and fled like she was the winner of British Bulldog.

# Tess

Tess came to, with a growing weird awareness that she'd not been conscious. Her blurred memory cleared slowly. She dimly grasped that she'd been in an accident and must've veered off the road. The sun was positioned high in the sky. She recalled that she and Rachel had set out for what was meant to be a nice drive before lunch, maybe at around eleven o'clock? Groaning in pain, a spasm of shock pulsed through her whole body with the accompanying realisation …

*Rachel. Where is Rachel!*

*Is she okay? Lord, help me! What if she isn't, okay?*

She pushed off the scratchy grey blanket weighted on her torso, and began to slowly crawl, calling out hoarsely. She struggled to get up but steadied herself on her hands and knees. She scoured the surrounding countryside, one hand shading her eyes from the glare. Desperation. The primal need to find her child obscured the pain of her injuries at that moment in time. She saw a flash of yellow out of place, low on the fence-line which bordered the steep incline to the base of the rocky outcrop; Budginigi Hill. For what seemed an interminable age, she stumbled towards it, panting.

Rachel's slipper was stuck in the hollow under the section of wire, where every Table-Top kid knows is the one place along the fence-line where a small frame will slip perfectly. Tess knew in a flash that if Rachel had run away scared, she would have sought the protection of the boulders and gullies she knew so well. Groaning and giddy, Tess pressed herself between the fence in search of her daughter, leaving her own skin and blood caught on the barbed wire.

*Trust your instincts!* A popular saying which often turned round and round in her brain, like a mouse on a wheel. Sometimes the intensity and constancy of her self-talk made her dizzy. Especially so, with a head injury. Not that instincts were always enough; she countered in her mind. In the past, she'd experienced flashes of insight where she saw her life careering out of control until it crashed; a vivid show she was powerless to stop.

*Typical,* she mused bitterly, while she dragged herself up the hill. She'd been laughing and singing with her child, then *wham*! Glass shattering. Oblivion. Tess continued to groggily berate herself. *How could she be so blindsided to believe in the goodness of life at that moment? So much for prescience when you really needed it!* Finally, she ceased, having scarce enough energy to use it in her tirade against herself. All she could do now was ride the surge of desperate instinct to find her child.

# Sarge

1

Table-Top's only policeman was in the office on this Tuesday afternoon, unaware yet of the dramatic events which had unfolded only a couple of kilometres away. He'd often come in much earlier to the office than needed. He liked the easy company of his secretary and the predictability of the day's routine. Like many blokes, he sometimes escaped into work when he felt powerless to navigate the expectations at home. Sarge admitted that he adored his wife yet struggled to stay in sync with her. For reasons unknown to him, he created a distance between them. Well, that's what his bride accused him of doing. *Guilty* as charged he reckoned. That which he could so easily say or do to convey his appreciation or love for her, Sarge all too often, messed up horribly.

Not so with his daughter Anna. No walls could withstand her innocent affection. He imagined that all kids had a way of ignoring the guard rails grown-ups erected, and smash through the carefully laid brickwork of self-protection and cynicism built over a lifetime. Anna, however, was an especially sweet child, who seemed oblivious to any potential barriers. Yep, grown women puzzled him at times, and he felt wary of the disappointment he sometimes saw veiled in the eyes of his wife. He knew that she loved him, and he loved her, yet he could never be sure that he was enough for her. His efforts to reach her were often clumsy and ill-timed. When it came to his own little girl however, she unreservedly showed her adoration for her dad, and he'd give her his soul if he thought it would bring her delight.

Giving up on the paperwork which he'd already abandoned in his reverie, he decided to make tea, which was an unspoken signal to Nancy to retrieve her latest crossword from her desk drawer. They sat in companionable silence for ten minutes.

"This is a tough one, Sarge. Mmm… Bet you can't give me a five-letter word for "a deceptive move?"

"Trick?"

"Nah."

"Ruse? Oh, wait - that's only four letters. Hmm…. can't say I have a clue," said Sarge, using a well-worn joke shared between him and the kindly office lady.

"Feint!" she pronounced triumphantly.

"Faint?" Sarge said dubiously, "What?"

"With an *e*, not an *a*, boss."

"Orright…like in boxing, I get it. It's a kind of a distraction… like when you feint with the right but swing with the left."

"Well, you have an advantage over me in the boxing department," chuckled Nancy. Sarge had been a pillar of the Police Boys Club and the boxing training program.

Nancy was craning her neck at an odd angle. "In all truth, I cheated to solve it. That's what the solutions are for, upside down in the back of the book."

The office telephone mercifully rang, breaking the monotony of the day. He didn't mind a mental challenge, but there's only so much Sarge could take when conversing about crossword clues.

Nancy laid the puzzle aside and cleared her throat, drawing herself up with dignity.

"Table Top Police Station. This is Nancy. How might I assist you today?"

She listened for a moment and caught Sarge's eye with a significant look. The policeman straightened himself, knowing by the unspoken communication that had passed between them, that an important police matter was being phoned in.

2

Sarge pulled up abruptly at the crash site in his standard issue police sedan. He allowed a moment for the great cloud of dust to settle before opening his door. He stilled himself and scanned the scene with a careful eye as his training had instilled in him. This was no single vehicle accident. Right away he recognised this car skewed across the wrong side of the road - over from the intersection of a little used laneway. His gaze rested on the drab blue vehicle. The passenger side showed evidence of impact of another vehicle. Leaving the lights of the police vehicle on to flash intermittently their warning, the officer approached the car, whistling low as he appreciated up close, the damage done to the side of Tess's Corolla.

His heart sinking, Sarge approached the car, the front-end angled slightly into the low ditch adjacent to the opposite lane of traffic. He indicated to the passerby who had slowed as he skirted the crashed vehicle on his side of the road, to keep moving on. Puzzled, the policeman scratched his head. His daughter had told him at breakfast that Rachel was home from school that week, feeling poorly. Yet there was no mother or child at the scene. Where the heck were they?

He opened the driver door carefully with gloved hands, poking his head inside. Wrinkling his nose and grimacing, he tried to ignore the pungent smell of smashed eggs fermenting in the intense noonday sun. He took in the fine, long hair caught in the edges of the shattered windscreen.

Straightening back up, he slowly scanned the area around the car, turning 360 degrees on the spot. No pretty, young woman, no blonde-headed child to be seen. No second vehicle. He circled the car carefully, noting a yellow slipper on the ground not far from the back passenger side door. On the driver's side he again noted the impact, looking vainly towards the side road. No skid marks whatsoever!

*Someone didn't bother to give way at the T- intersection!*

*Nor did they bother to stick-around,* he muttered to himself.

As he neared the front of the car again, glass crunched under the thick leather soles of his police boots. He observed the dent on the bonnet and shuddered when he realised it must've been made by Tess as she was flung out of the front window. Gingerly, he inspected the pool of blood where she must have landed on the ground, metres away. Momentum was not one's friend in these sorts of circumstances. *Strange-* he notes an old grey blanket which lies crumpled at the site with blood congealing on it. Again, Sarge scanned the scene.

*Tess! Rachel!* He called loudly with intermittent whistles.

Tracing the trail back to the main pool of blood and the blanket -which looked like it had been tossed aside by a sleeper on an unusually hot night- he called out again. Each time he called he waited and listened, eyes roaming the dry surrounds for any movement. Taking his time and with great care with where he placed his feet, he followed smears and spots of blood across the road and then onto the dry yellow grass up the incline to the fence at the base of Budginigi Reserve. Going back to the passenger door which remained open, he examined the area for signs of blood in what must have been Rachel's seat. Sarge breathed a sigh of relief – there was none.

Sarge returned to his vehicle and reached for the two-way radio. He communicated the licence plate, name of the assumed driver and the request for back-up to Albury Police Station. Curtly, he gave the identity and description of the missing child. HQ would alert Highway Patrol. Sarge then patched through the request for an ambulance to be on stand-by. He contacted Nancy at the local switchboard and instructed her to contact the principal of Table Top School and confirm that Rachel Moloney was indeed absent school from today and in the care of her mum- and to arrange a current school photo of child to be dropped into the station as a matter of urgency.

"Get onto the RFS please, Nancy. We need to put the call out for volunteers for search and rescue. We're either dealing with an abduction of a child, or a lost child, plus a missing and seriously injured mother."

Taking a moment to mop his brow, the policeman momentarily struggled with his personal feelings, steeling himself and regaining his professional demeanour.

3

The chopper was deafening as it swept over the search party that was gathering at the base of Budginigi, everyone holding onto their hats and maps in the updraft.

"Time is critical. We only have three hours of good daylight left," barked Sarge at the rabble of local farmers and parents of Rachel's classmates who had gladly volunteered their help. Small communities like this always pulled together in a crisis.

"Now, most of you know the facts at hand. We have a highly irregular situation. Tess and Rachel Moloney are victims of what appears to be a hit and run incident. Not only is the other driver AWOL, but both mother and daughter are missing from the scene. We don't know if the child was injured in the crash, but we do know that at least she wasn't bleeding. However, she's already sick and being treated for mumps. We don't even know categorically that she wasn't abducted. A child's slipper was found by the car and a second slipper has been located at the fence line between Budginigi and the road below us, indicating that Rachel Moloney may've headed to the hill for refuge. Did she hide? Did she make it to cover? Why was she so frightened? Was someone chasing her? All questions we don't have answers to."

Sarge paused to let this information sink in for his audience.

"Highway Patrol are doing spot-searches on cars in the vicinity, but it's the proverbial *needle in a haystack*. At best, mother and child have left the crash scene - Tess badly injured. At worst, the perpetrator has one or both of 'em."

There was a surge of murmuring in the assembled group. Whistles of surprise, amid mutterings of "they might be stuffed," and the like, could be heard around the gathering of men. Many of the volunteers had hardened exteriors which belied their soft hearts.

Sarge continued grimly, "Our initial investigations *do* point to the child wandering away from the scene, or fleeing in fear, as likely scenarios, so we need to put our resources into a thorough search of the area. We can't rule out an abduction entirely, we can't rule out yet that the *perp* did not chase her and catch her. We just don't know at this stage. The abduction line of inquiry is being handled by a dedicated task force. But we have a job to do here. Our role now is vital. We are operating under a working theory that the child and mother are possibly nearby, needing our help. It is likely that they left the scene at different times. Blood spots have been sighted, presumably Tess's - who possibly went after the little one at some point. We don't have all the information we would like, but what we can do is to use the remaining hours of daylight to gather whatever evidence there is on the hill and hope and pray that we have a good outcome. We're hoping at this stage that the driver of the other vehicle has done his worst and poses no further risk of harm to the mother and child. It appears that even though he was at fault, a fact compounded by fleeing the scene, he did cover Tess with a blanket to presumably offset symptoms of shock from the accident. We know that Tess was thrown clear of the car and can't be in a good way. She presumably lay on the road for a spell given the blood pool there."

Sarge shook his head in frustration and cleared his throat.

"Tess was ejected from the vehicle through the windscreen, upon impact. It's possible that she woke disoriented and dragged herself off… looking for her daughter."

As each revelation was imparted, there was a rising murmur in unison amongst the assembled volunteers.

"Bugger, that would be about right," one dairy farmer uttered.

"Tess was pretty slack about wearing a seatbelt!" another declared.

"There are lots of places that a woman or child could run into trouble up yonder, especially if they were hurt or frightened," a weathered face in front of the policeman pointed out.

There was much agreement among the assembled crew.

"Goes without saying that finding both the missing child and mother is our immediate priority. The Albury Crime team are focusing on the crash scene itself and gathering forensic evidence, so please do not interfere with their investigation on the road. It falls to us here, who know the area and the victims, to locate Tess and Rachel before nightfall. Today. I don't care about that low life who left the scene… and *left them…* just yet. Police will track the other driver down in due course. We can only hope! Hospitals and local doctor's surgeries have been alerted in case he presents for medical attention himself. Hear me. Our job now is to focus our efforts on finding a frightened child and a mum, who must be pretty banged-up from the accident."

Sarge scratched the stubble on his chin.

"Look, my hunch is that they could well be nearby. Rachel Moloney, like many of the Table Top tribe, knows this area like the back of her hands. We have a window of opportunity to find Tess and Rachel if they are in this immediate area, while the light holds. Can I repeat, you need to concentrate as you go about the search. It is vital that you tread carefully, and bag anything you think could be evidence. Keep chatter to a minimum. Be looking and listening. Call out their names regularly, but make sure that you stop and listen for a response. Use the whistles you've been given to alert Tom if you find anything."

Sarge nodded at Tom. He tipped his hat back.

"Please raise your hand, those of you who have a two-way radio."

Sarge waited for the group to note those with raised hands.

"Look around gents. Let one of these guys know if you have information. Godspeed everyone. Pass on your findings to myself or to your Squad Captain. Over to you, Tom."

At that, the RFS captain subdivided the crowd and assigned them to their designated search areas. Intermittent sounds of *'Cooee!'* and the names of the missing pair bounced off walls of rock.

4

An hour passed and there was no news. Then another hour, and another. The afternoon wore on. Sarge made a quick trip back down the hill at around 5:00 p.m. to the car radio for some quick comms. It'd been confirmed that the Moloney mum and daughter weren't currently at their property, and so assumed that they were indeed the occupants of the crashed Corolla. Highway patrol hadn't uncovered any leads indicative of the mother and daughter being abducted. No one had turned themselves in at either the Table-Top or Albury police stations. Other than the initial alert that there had been an accident, Nancy hadn't yet received any community calls, anonymous or otherwise, with information which may have been helpful to the investigation. The media were calling, of course. Nothing else.

*A whole lot of nothing,* muttered Sarge, under his breath, as he slammed down the receiver and kicked the tire. The policeman, always doggedly thorough, then picked up the radio handset again and instructed Nancy to patch through a direct call to the school principal, Mr Holden. They spoke for a good ten minutes about his understanding of Rachel's personality and how he thought things had been going at home. The Sergeant knew the child a little, of course, but he wanted to get her teacher's insights into her personality and gain a sense of what Rachel might be capable of in a crisis. Holden's perception was that Rachel was a resilient child, somewhat wary of adults and slow to trust, but once comfortable in her environment, she was very animated, fun-loving, musical and imaginative. Rachel loved the routines and stimulation of school. She was both book-smart and street-smart; a combination you rarely saw in a child not yet out of primary school. Whilst in no way rubbishing Tess's parenting, the teacher did allude to Rachel Moloney perhaps having seen a bit more of life than the average child had.

The Police Sergeant felt the pressure building; there was less than two hours of light left. How could the two just vanish?

*C'mon Tess, c'mon Rachel. Where are you?*

He puffed up the slope, yet again.

Then came the breakthrough they desperately needed. The radio clipped to his belt sounded. It was Tom.

"You're gonna wanna come and see this, Sarge."

"At last!" Sarge continued round the hill panting. He veered off to the western side of the outcrop as directed. The report he'd received was the sighting of a child's stuffed toy elephant. It was found propped against a rock with dried lichen, like a sentry, on look-out. Out of place, yet a very welcome sight. The toy hadn't been weathered by dew or dust but looked like only moments ago it could have been arranged by a child in play. An excited volunteer had carefully bagged the find, placing a marker in its place and sharing the news of the find with Captain Tom, as soon as he could access a two-way radio.

Finally, a fresh clue! Sarge was forced down the hill again to wait impatiently at his police vehicle while Nancy at the switchboard contacted his wife Sarah, to ask Anna if an elephant was part of Rachel's stuffed animal menagerie.

Anna, who had been eating milk and cookies at the kitchen table with her mum, was able to confirm with huge solemn eyes, that "Ellie" was one of Rachel's favourite toys.

This development confirmed the policeman's gut instinct that Rachel, and hopefully her mother, were nearby after all. The news was passed quietly, but urgently, amongst all the men, like the childhood game of Chinese whispers. Yet another half-hour passed, with no fresh discoveries.

5

Sarge chewed his lip in concentration. He just might have the beginnings of an idea.

*See things through the eyes of a child*, he admonished himself. What was it that the school teacher had said? Rachel Moloney responded to music like the Pied Piper himself was calling her. She particularly loved the *Let's Sing* sessions which Mr Holden held after lunch on Thursdays. Gotta hand it to him, thought Sarge, for an uptight teaching principal, Holden was pretty engaging with the children. Good with the guitar too, and he had a passable singing voice. Sarge's own daughter Anna, continually chattered to him about the songs they'd do each week. She'd only mentioned to her dad, just last week, how much she and Rachel shared a love of these relaxing afternoon sing sessions. The girls were inseparable anyway, but they looked forward to *Let's Sing* together with a passion. Anna had even insisted that she teach her dad her latest favourite song.

When it came to his daughter, the burley police officer was as soft and gooey as the trifle his dear mother had made every Christmas. Laced with generous portions of sherry, it produced a sense of relaxed contentment when consumed. Sarge was equally compliant when it came to interactions with his daughter. It had been like this since the day she was born. After a complicated labour, he and Sarah had endured an all-night vigil waiting for her to be born by Caesarean Section first thing the following morning. When Anna was delivered the paediatrician brought the squalling newborn over to him.

"See this?" He had said, motioning for him to look at Anna's tiny fist. Understandably, as a new father, Sarge had momentarily panicked, his mind racing ahead, imagining some medical problem or God forbid, a deformity! The doctor carefully unpeeled an exquisite, minuscule little finger.

"You my friend, are going to be wrapped around this for the rest of your life."

*Indeed,* Sarge had thought, as he'd relaxed again. There was an unmistakable twinkle in the doc's eye, not obscured by the mask and scrubs which festooned him. As predicted from the day of her birth, Sarge did find it difficult to refuse Anna anything. So, when she'd seemed so delighted to teach him a song- he couldn't resist her contagious joy, and he obediently became her attentive pupil.

Sarge tripped on a tree root as he trudged along. Back in the present moment, he racked his brain for the latest song Anna had been singing around the house (and had him join in on).

"World of our Own!" he said to himself in triumph.

At least it was a decent song in its own right - not like some of the inane kiddy songs he had suffered through in Anna's toddler years. Instead of routinely calling Rachel and Tess by name, he began to hum the *Seekers* hit song as he searched. After a bit, he gained enough momentum to remember both the lyrics and tune at the same time. He ruefully congratulated himself on this small achievement. Repeatedly, as he trudged the skinny path, he crooned in rumblings of baritone, snatches of song which ricocheted off the rocks around him …

*Close the door, light the light*
*We're stayin' home tonight*
*Far away from the bustle and the bright city lights*
*Let them all fade away, just leave us alone…*

As Sarge trudged through a small ravine in the transcendent afternoon light, he spied a flash of white gold, which heightened his senses to full alert. Did he imagine that? Were his eyes playing tricks on him in the luminous light bathing the landscape? Could that have been a golden head darting out from cover, that he'd spotted out of the corner of his eye? A sight more precious in this moment than the exchange of golden wedding bands between any passionate couple.

Then, as his heart expanded, a tiny face emerged from under a time-worn rocky overhang. A small child unfolded herself from her hiding place, her cow and moon pyjamas becoming increasingly visible. She stood warily looking at him. Sarge kept crooning the song. Crouching down, he slowly reached one arm forward, palm-up in gentle invitation with his outstretched hand. The child solemnly regarded him without making a sound. Her intense stillness a sure sign that she was poised for flight. The gap between them seemed to widen, the longer the moment of indecision stretched out. Then in an instant, the child ran forward, took his hand and fixed her wide solemn eyes on his face. Rachel Moloney halted in front of him and pointed shyly to the canteen of water he had attached to his belt. Gently he helped her guzzle the water like a lamb just weaned from its mother. Soft soothing sounds unconsciously bubbled from the policeman's lips, unrecognisable to himself. Very, very slowly, the policeman extended his arms around the quivering child. He drew her into his chest and felt the tension go out of her body. Rachel held his gaze for one long moment as they knelt there in the fast-fading light. He lifted her up. She settled her head onto his shoulder as he secured her on his hip. Snuggling in, she sniffed his crisp, ironed shirt and was comforted.

Rachel succumbed to sleep before Sarge had finished adjusting his Walkie-Talkie back on his belt. Exhaustion, sickness, shock and fright all combined as she fell fast asleep in that way that children do and adult's envy. No longer needing to be hyper-vigilant, Rachel rested.

Whoops of delights could be heard reverberating around the hills as the message spread that the child had finally been found. Exhilaration. Search and rescue teams can never fully put into words that sensation of finding the lost. None of the exuberance roused Rachel.

# Tess

1

But where was Tess? Blood had been sighted in multiple locations on the way up the hill by the willing search crew. A small sticky patch had been found on the fence wire, along with the distinct long, light strand of hair.

*Gotta hand it to the locals,* thought Sarge. They might look like a motley crew, but you couldn't say that any one of them didn't have a sharp eye and gritty determination. He'd handed the search crew over to capable Tom Elder while he rested a spell and kept close by the little one, he had triumphantly retrieved as she hid under the overhang of the rock. The paramedics had wrapped her up warmly and were performing their routine medical checks ahead of her transportation to Albury Base Hospital for further tests and observation. Sarge watched the fresh search party as they passed, armed with torches-in hand and helmets on heads. He uttered his thanks that Rachel was spared from being alone up there in the darkness.

Poor Tess, though. Tom was heading up the next shift of volunteers from the Rural Fire Service. He was the squad captain, but also the father of a large family, and hence, most of the kids at Table Top Central School. This search for the missing mum was personal for him.

Tom had grimly reminded the team, as per Sarge's instructions, that time was of the essence to find Tess. The accident scene told a grim tale. Evidence of the driver being thrown from the vehicle was patent. The pool of blood near the blanket indicated that Tess had laid motionless for some time. It was thought that once the mother had come to, she had scrambled away to look for her daughter. The school teacher, who was now helping with the search, was emphatic that they find the mother before nightfall. He and everyone knew that the risks of wandering around the bush at day were bad enough, let alone at nighttime.

"I don't like her chances!" he said.

The squad leader had made it clear that any such harbinger of doom was premature. Sarge admired the way that Tom capably and quietly kept the crew focused and positive.

Frustratingly, Sarge had been unable to get anything out of Rachel. She seemed to have lost her power of speech and would only shake her head sadly when asked if she knew where her mother was. The only response Sarge received when he gently asked her who the other driver might be was a tight-lipped expression, as Rachel watched him cagily.

*Lord knows the child would chatter like a magpie when she was visiting with Anna.*

The trauma of what she'd experienced, combined with her sky-high temperature, succeeded in overwhelming Rachel. She'd been unwilling to be parted from her burly rescuer too. Waking when the ambos were checking her out on the stretcher, she'd grabbed the policeman's arm as he sat next to her and held on for dear life. Sarge sat wedged in the uncomfortable seat adjacent to the patient, while the ambulance was stationary. Not surprisingly, he made the decision to travel into Albury Base Hospital, knowing that was where he needed to be, now. He unreservedly trusted the team left behind on the hills. The ambulance rumbled along for the twenty-five minutes it took to get into Albury. Sarge brought up the rear.

2

At Table Top, the light changed to a deeper sepia with rays of the setting sun occasionally dazzling the searchers as they encountered cracks between towering rock faces. In this part of the country, the twilight gloaming hung suspended in time for longer than expected, but then ended as abruptly as a false promise, when the sun finally dipped below the horizon.

Torches were utilised, and a thorough search made of every crevice and behind every boulder, near the location Rachel had been hiding in. It was just a precaution. It stood to reason that if Rachel knew where her Mum was, she would've indicated where Tess was- but the volunteers searched the overhang and surrounds, regardless. It quickly became expedient to pull the teams out before someone slipped and broke their ankle or fell of the side of a cliff. There were just too many ravines and rabbit holes. The men called and listened, listened and called. Tom even shouted to the silence the news that Rachel had been found; and that Tess need only focus on getting help for herself.

The men slowly gathered next to the road. The chopper did a final sweep, and the men held onto their now redundant hats- grass animated momentarily- until the helicopter changed direction and *whirred* back to Sydney. It was with a heavy heart that Tom called the search off 'til first light.

Tom was the last to leave, speaking firmly, though it felt like only the stars and the wind witnessed his message,

"Hang in there Tess Moloney! We're not giving up. You have a little girl who needs you. See you in the morning."

# Sarge

1

All in all, it was a more interesting Tuesday than usual, Sarge could only conclude. A routine day had morphed into the biggest day of policing that he'd encountered since he accepted the post to Table Top. Sarge reckoned that attending the crash scene and later succeeding in flushing out young Rachel from her hiding spot, was as good a day's work as he'd ever had.

"Poor little mite," he had said to Sarah as he'd crawled into bed late that night. She'd waited up, but then finally retired, leaving her bedside lamp on so he'd know that she was expecting him to wake her up when he got in for the night.

"Pretty relieved I am at that. Thank the Lord, Rachel felt comfortable enough to come out of her hiding spot, to me. If that was our daughter in that situation… well, it doesn't bear thinking about. What a relief! I'm so glad I can tell Anna that her buddy is safe and sound, when she wakes in the morning."

"Wonderful news, darling. Let's hope tomorrow brings good news about Tess too."

"Hmm… it's hard to turn-in, knowing that Tess is still out there. I like her. I don't believe all the gossip. Not sure why she is estranged from her family. No doubt Tess has had a tough run, but it seems to me she was doing her best with her kid. Who knows what Rachel Moloney has seen or experienced before this? But she still needs her Mum to be okay."

Sarah squeezed her husband's hand in response.

"Rachel has this vulnerability combined with wise older eyes… can't quite put my finger on it. Sad that she doesn't have a decent dad around. Guess I have a soft spot for her … couldn't do much more for her at the hospital, or I would have stayed even longer." Sarge's chatter petered off as he yawned. The day's adrenaline was subsiding, and weariness crept in to take its place. "Tom's a capable bloke… I'm sure he will find Tess if she's up there… hopefully… alive…" Sarge started to drowse off, one hand flung protectively over his wife's abdomen.

Sarah kissed her husband on the forehead tenderly. "Even heroes have to sleep and come home to their own families," she murmured.


2


Sarge abruptly but not unpleasantly, woke well after sun-up. Anna enthusiastically launched herself at him. With great delight, Sarge told his daughter that he'd succeeded in finding Rachel. Anna wormed her way under the covers and, turning her back to him, spooned her warm little body - clad in cosy flannelette pyjamas - close to him. He relished her snuggling into him, pulling her close to his chest and resting his chin on her soft head. He inhaled the sweet smell of his child's hair, the freshness of childhood. At his back, he was very aware of his wife's close contact, her hand resting on his shoulder, completing this precious moment with all who were dear to him. He knew he had a lot to be grateful for.

He lingered in the moment as long as he could, but all too soon he was forced to break the spell and rise for the day. He was required to attend Albury

Police station, and he had yet to write up his report. Maybe there would be fresh intel, what with the activation of the wider community who had been alerted by numerous radio and television reports to be on the lookout for the perpetrator of the hit-and- run accident.

Sarge felt torn. He knew he needed to fulfil his administrative and leadership duties, but he found it difficult not to be on the ground helping with the search for Tess Moloney. He reassured himself with the knowledge that the man in charge of the volunteer search crew, Tom Elder, was a quiet, capable man with invaluable local knowledge. His property backed onto the foot of the Budginigi Hills.

Slamming his door shut in the car park at Albury Police Station, Sarge straightened his uniform. The street boasted a line of ancient and stately plane trees, so he took a moment to gather his thoughts under the protective shade they provided. He always enjoyed attending both the historic courthouse and station house, in this beautiful, old part of town.

The priority which he felt important to communicate to his superiors, was that they needed to continue with the media releases. He wanted people in their homes up and down the Riverina, to know as they ate their cornflakes and scrambled eggs, to be on the lookout for a damaged white vehicle. The most rudimentary forensics survey at the scene had identified white paint scrapings on the blue front end of Tess Moloney's car. It was unlikely that the offender had taken Tess with him when he fled the scene as the blood pool indicated Tess had remained there for some time, and the blanket indicated the driver has made some effort to mitigate shock before he left Tess there.

The ridiculous thing was that whilst the driver of the other vehicle was at fault (anyone approaching a T- Intersection is required to give way by law), he was not responsible for the likely severity of the mother's injuries. These were caused by her failure to wear a seat belt. Why such a panic? Unless the driver already had something to lose or was already known to police?

Checking that his hat was straight in the reflection of the car window one last time, the police officer hastened into the city station. The duty officer at the front desk welcomed Sarge with a grin and with the news that a message had been left that would interest him. Sarge thanked him and quickly scanned the phone record.

An anonymous call had come in indicating a damaged white ute which been sighted, with Victorian number plates, getting petrol near the Table Top Tourist Park. The note said that the male caller hung up quickly, but there was one other detail included on the document- the voice providing the anonymous tip-off seemed young and that someone much older in the background was coaching him

"Well, that would have been a useful tip to be able to follow up, if the caller had allowed it!" retorted Sarge. "Blast! What's wrong with people these days? Would it kill them to put a name to their info? What have they got to hide?"

"You've got no argument from me, Sir," said the desk officer with a shrug, shifting his attention to the stacked paper tower on his desk, which threatened to topple over at the smallest provocation.

Sarge pulled himself together before he went into his meeting. He didn't forget to thank the bearer of bad news.

# Tess

## 1

The night Rachel was taken to hospital, and Sarge had returned to his family, Tom Elder's mind never strayed far from the search (and much hoped for rescue) of Tess Moloney which he would be coordinating at sun-up. There was such jubilation when Rachel was rescued, but the night ahead wasn't going to be an easy one for many locals, with Tess's location yet to be discovered.

Preoccupied, Tom assisted his capable wife with the intense nightly routine which belonged to his large family. He was sharply aware that while he participated in domestic life, in chores that were simple pleasures, Tess Moloney was alone and hurt, lying who-knows-where outdoors. He picked up toys, retrieved school shoes, and checked backpacks for rotting fruit. When he tucked his own children into bed, kissing their brows and safely securing their comfort blanket or teddy, he breathed a prayer of gratitude that Rachel at least, had been rescued before nightfall.

He was too on edge to settle down for the night, so when the missus, and finally, even the older kids had retired, Tom Elder retreated to his dusty office. It was only an alcove off the dining room, but it provided him with a cramped two by two metres of space, which was all his own in a bustling, bursting household. His wife and children had little interest in his office, but his four-legged companion loved to squeeze into the space.

He pushed aside some farm invoices piling up and clinked on his lamp. He was the third generation of Elders to farm his patch which was just on the other side of the hills where the day's drama had unfolded. Sinking into his sagging leather chair, weary but wired, he reviewed the facts of the situation, his brow furrowed in concentration. He didn't move for a long time.

Physically he was spent, with the search coming on top of the perpetual farm chores. He stretched his aching muscles. Something was nagging him on the periphery of his mind. He sat and sat. Eventually hunger drove him to hunt and devour some leftovers in the fridge. He settled back into his chair again, nursing a cuppa on his knee, but then suddenly jerked forward, sloshing the now cold tea onto his weathered hand. Wiping himself on the bottom of his shirt he battled with a stubborn drawer in his filing cabinet. He pulled out a faded map. Unfurled, he began to pore over it under lamplight.

"Tess can't have disappeared off the face of the blasted earth," he said abruptly.

At the sound of his voice, his faithful dog raised her head from resting on her paws from the corner where she had been napping. Terri the terrier looked at his master quizzically. She may not have been given the most inventive name, but she was a good ol' companion.

"Ah, but she could!" he burst out again, with a gleam of hope in his eye. This time he made eye contact for the benefit of Terri, who seemed to understand him better than people sometimes.

Finally, Tom made moves to turn in for the few hours which remained of the dark. He muttered a short sharp prayer upward, grimly hoping that like a well-placed arrow, his supplication had hit its mark.

2

Well before first light, Tom was up and ready. He wasted no time. He hurriedly dressed and had breakfast. Nonetheless he didn't take any short cuts as he expertly checked and repacked his rucksack ensuring that dehydrated food, electrolytes, torch, a first-aid kit and foil blanket, were all in order. Years of experience of heading up search and rescue in the upper Murray area and attending way too many bushfires than he cared to count, had schooled him well in his preparation. He'd searched for several lost or injured hikers in his time, but never had he been looking for the victims of a hit -and- run crash where the victims as well as the offender had all taken off!

Elder was rewarded for his efficient efforts when he pulled up in his Rural Fire Service truck on the road adjacent to the base of *Big Budgi,* with the arrival of the first rays of sun, rising from behind the ridge - a most welcome, punctual guest. The looming hills began to materialise from the morning mist. Clipping his *Leather-man,* canteen and two-way radio onto his belt, he whistled for the dog on the back of the ute. Well-trained and obedient, Terri had been eagerly awaiting his signal. Captain Elder paced next to the wooden picnic table situated just past the fence line, which was the agreed rendezvous point for the crew to come. He'd only had to wait a few minutes before the local volunteers quietly arrived from different directions. Many of the men and women looked as though they had slept as little as he had.

Tom huddled with the first wave of the RFS volunteers and left one capable crew member to brief the next lot of searchers to arrive. He led his team up the slope with a careful but determined tread. They skirted the base of the immediate hill of rocks before them and moved north-east towards a stand of ironbark which lay between the big and little hills. *Little Budgi* still had an elevation of at least 250 metres, but visitors tended to mainly explore the bigger hill that was more easily accessed from Mitchell Road.

He was very familiar with these two humble hills nestled into the Great Dividing Range, between Table-Top and Ettamogah. His own property was closer to Table Top Mountain via road, but on foot he could easily walk to this site from the rear of his property. Whilst historically, his family had never held the biggest land holding, unlike the Mitchell family, for which the nearby road had been named, the Elders knew the whole area intimately.

He had encouraged himself and the RFS crew at the quick morning briefing, reminding them that yesterday they had succeeded in finding Rachel before dark; today was the day to find Tess Moloney, before she had to endure another night outside. Search and Rescue never entertained the possibility that they were searching for anything other than a live missing-person, in the first forty-eight hours of a job.

Trudging along, Tom was wrapped in his thoughts. He and his men, as per protocol, had fanned out over an extensive area. Tom didn't even want to imagine what it would've been like if the little one had not crept out of her hiding place last night… or what it would be like if one of his own kids was lost overnight. He grimaced involuntarily. *Heck!* The youngest of his brood still insisted that a night light be left on in the hallway, and they were capable farm kids. His children, just like he as a child, had started steering the tractor when the stock was fed grain, from the tender age of four or five. There were many grown-up tasks the kids assisted with on the farm, but to-date, there had only ever been minor mishaps. The kids emerged undaunted, boasting about each adventure. That said, darkness, cold and being alone were another thing all together. Not that any adults he knew were a huge fan of this combination either.

*Tess Moloney had likely landed the trifecta,* he reflected grimly.

As RFS Group Captain, Sarge had briefed Elder that the initial forensics assessment of the scene indicated that the offending driver had fled the crime scene alone. The Police were operating under a working hypothesis that at different points in time, the mother and child each ran away from the road to the security of the rocky incline. There were no footprints or drag marks to suggest that the injured mum had unwillingly or willingly entered the other vehicle. Tess could not have ascended far up the hill given the state she would have been in. The blood trail did not support it. Logically, she should have been found before the child was located. He reckoned she would have skirted around the hill, on a lower path.

*Where are you, Tess?*

He paused and checked his map. Exhaling softly, he covered the short distance to the area he had encircled with a stubby pencil the night before.

In years past, both Budginigi hills had been exploited to produce the road-fill required for the construction of a new highway, when the council decided that the road needed to be raised. Later generations might de-stock and re-tree the area, but at the present, the hills and surrounds were entirely bereft of topsoil under the scrub.

Tom Elder remembered as a young man, the rumours of an old station-hand, who had claimed that there existed a hidden crater made by a past dynamite blast.

"Mind how you go," he had warned Tom as they had yarned one night after a big day of sheep- marking. The old fella, gnarled by decades of back-breaking work, but tough as leather, had ruminated that the crater was screened by one of the numerous rock clusters, north of the tree line which separated the hills of *Big* and *Little Budgi*.

Tom checked the grid references twice from the cross-section of the map he'd identified for investigation the night previous. The RFS Captain hoped upon hope that his idea was correct and that he'd rightly narrowed the search area.

*Oh, that the earth might offer Tess as first fruits of the new day!*

Yet the morning light grew with no leads and as the sun climbed higher and higher, millions of flecks of minerals embedded in the rock, sparkled. Methodically, he and the men who had rejoined him, after eliminating their own assigned area, arduously searched behind, around, and even under the many groupings of scrubby shrubs and speckled rock formations, topped with brittle moss.

Each man chalked each grouping on the ground once it was searched, to prevent them from doubling-up. One of the men swore and grumbled that Tom was "off his rocker."

Another volunteer cheerfully contributed, "Needle in a haystack, mate!"

A Kelpie belonging to a volunteer happily lolled back and forth between the men. The terrier marched ahead as top dog, but Terri stuck her head down as many rabbit holes as she could as they searched.

This routine went on and on until late morning. Elder stopped to rest a spell, when he decided it was time to remove a layer of clothing. Pressing his back against a towering boulder, he took a swig from his canteen. Rearranging his rucksack, he went to head off again. As he rounded the huge boulder, he was dazzled by the sun which had risen high in the sky. Cursing, he tripped and fell heavily. Rubbing his shin in pain, he inspected the ground to see what he stumbled over so stupidly.

*Ah!*

A rusted shovel scoop protruded from the earth, a leftover from the era when workers crawled over the *Budgi* hills extracting truckload after truckload (from countless, sweaty barrow loads) of mineral and stone particles, to be compacted under today's interstate highway.

Terri sniffed around Tom, briefly licking his hand in sympathy. The dog ditched him quick enough though, proving very distracted by something behind him. Tom clambered up and went to inspect whatever it was which so fascinated the pup. Possibly, she'd discovered a colony of rabbits. Terri was still, one paw lifted and frozen in time, only a slight twitching of her nose breaking her pose.

"Whatcha' looking at *gel*?" he crooned to the Terrier.

She began to bark excitedly, poking her nose through the scrub nearby. In the next instance, all but her back legs were visible with the stub of a tail quivering with glee. Then, in a matter of seconds, Terri disappeared entirely from view. A strange, muffled bark rang out.

Tom removed the whistle attached to his belt, and instinctively sounded the alert. Hacking away at the bushes with a small machete, he stopped short suddenly when he realised that the ground sloped downwards dramatically. Otherwise, he risked tumbling headfirst into a large hole that he could now see opened before him. Shining his torch to and fro, he could just make out a drop of at least two metres below him. He sucked his breath in sharply. Adrenaline spiked in his veins. The powerful beam competed with a swarm of dust particles but succeeded in illuminating somewhat, the large, previously concealed cavity. Eventually Tom's eyes adjusted as he poked his head as far in as he dared.

There was Terri, dutifully guarding the petite frame of a crumpled woman, face down, with soft long hair streaming from the back of her head, marred by inroads of blood catching the torch light.

He yelled terse instructions at two of the first responders to his whistle communication, to shine their light through the mallee bush he had cleared. Lying flat on his stomach, Elder scooted round and carefully lowered himself down feet first. Gently he dropped down near the odd pair below, the dog guarding her find patiently, the woman, motionless. On hands and knees Tom crawled forward, grunting as he knocked his leg on more rusty metal. He reached down and felt blood. A tetanus booster was going to be mandatory now.

Tom Elder reached over the immobile woman, gingerly rolling down a section of her high-necked sweater. He placed two fingers at the side of her throat. He detected a faint pulse. He took a massive gulp of air, not even realising that he'd been holding his breath. He gave thanks, Tess was alive - just!

3

"The needle in the haystack's been found!" grinned Tom to the crew as they surveyed the paramedics strapping Tess onto the waiting, wheeled stretcher.

"Freak thing!" exclaimed one grimy volunteer.

"We thought she was done for," chimed another.

"She's safe now… well, I hope so, anyways."

The men murmured appreciatively, while passing the banter between them.

"This crater was made by dynamite-blast decades ago!"

"The luck of the Irish as they say! Fancy that - Tess Moloney managing to fall backwards into a forgotten enormous hole… and on top of that, to hit her head on remnants of a broken shovel! The blinkin' rusty article was likely left behind from the 1950s. These hills are pretty much the backbone of the Hume Highway build, you know?"

The men all nodded

"All this you see around you is minus its topsoil" Tom went on.

"Yep, they blasted it to buggery and carted rock and minerals big time in this area."

"If it hadn't been for the old maps in my office, which my old man kept updated, we wouldn't have found her, I wager. Reckon the good Lord Himself, reminded me." Tom asserted quietly.

"Not to forget Terri's help."

"Yep, He can use animals as well as humans," agreed Tom.

One old-timer continued to scratch the pleased terrier around her ears.

"Good thing you are a praying man, Elder, Tess is gonna need all the help she can get."

"She's not out of the woods yet."

The RFS volunteers had done their part. Now, they could enjoy the luxury of standing back and swapping stories.

It had been difficult getting the crumpled woman out of the hidden cavity, in such an inflexible position. Tom had assisted the paramedic who had scrambled down into the large subterranean space with a backpack filled with life-saving articles. The opening of the crater had become increasingly obvious once it had been discovered and accessed, and more and more of the scrub which had concealed the entrance, cut back. The capable ambulance officer had checked Tess's vital signs and splinted her neck as a precaution. His main concern was to get her out so that she could receive more extensive medical attention, as soon as possible.

Even though Tom was surrounded by shadows, everything he saw was vividly etched in his mind. He felt like an archaeologist who had uncovered precious ancient treasure. In his state of hyper-vigilance, Tom had noticed an inquisitive Gecko scratching along the entrance, which stationed itself in the corner, so that Tom could see its head and torso poking through the opening, its tail, no doubt still in the sunlight. The creature easily gripped the downside of the chamber, giving a realistic impression of a concerned onlooker taking in the scene: marsupials busily tending to one of their own and clumsily scrambling out of the giant burrow. Tom reckoned that having claws would have been very handy in this situation. Every precaution was taken to protect the patient from spinal damage or cranial injury.

The men grew quiet to appreciate the moment when the ambulance pulled away, lights flashing. The day was not done until the crew stopped off at the nearest watering hole for a well-earned beer, which the publican insisted was on the house. They allowed themselves an hour or so to take pleasure in reliving moments of the day and swapping stories of past rescues. It was very satisfying to celebrate the rescue of both mother and daughter. Slapping each other on the back, and toasting Tom, they embodied all that was loveliest about living in a small community. Newcomers sometimes found it all a bit suffocating, but could not dispute that in a pinch, Table Top pulled together like few places did. Good hearted, decent country folk, who rallied together to help a neighbour in need, no thought for their own agendas, personal prejudice pushed aside.

The men began to melt away before long. Each had animals to feed up or neglected chores to attend to. Many wanted to kiss their spouses and play with their kids, reminded of how precious it was to have their loved ones home safe and waiting for them. The last twenty-four hours had been intense for all the volunteers and their families. Scarcely anyone in the Table Top postcode was unaffected. Some had children at the school, and others were part of rescue efforts, or related to someone who was.

The entire community, having tensed together, now gave a collective sigh of relief. Almost. Tess was rescued, but her recovery wasn't yet sure. The child by all reports had not said *boo* to anyone. The culprit of the hit-and-run remained at large. Still, it was a good outcome so far. The community would go on being neighbourly like regular folks, but what happened next was largely out of their hands. Medical experts and the police force had a way to go yet.

After a trip to the clinic for his tetanus shot, Tom succumbed to exhaustion. He slept heavily. He struggled to stir himself until well after sun-up, as if he was waking from hibernation. After a shower and black coffee, he rang the Albury Base Hospital switchboard. The operator abandoned protocol and updated the caller. To the wiry farmer's immense satisfaction, he learned that Tess had lived through the night.

4

Tess Moloney regained consciousness in the early hours of Thursday morning, after being rehydrated after her ordeal. Her voice croaked when she attempted to call out and enquire after Rachel; she was weak and distressed. An Albury policewoman had been stationed inside the door, ready for this eventuality. She quickly placed herself at Tess's bedside and quietly briefed Tess in a factual, yet compassionate manner. Tess's eyes grew larger and larger as she learned that she'd been in an accident; it was believed that she'd left the scene disoriented, looking for her daughter, where she sustained a second serious head injury after a fall. The competent policewoman reassured Tess again and again that Rachel had been located ahead of her and remained relatively unscathed, considering she'd been in an accident, in the bush alone, all whilst battling Mumps, shock and dehydration. The officer didn't sugarcoat the truth that it was with some difficulty that the medical team had recently, finally brought Rachel's temperature down and she was resting comfortably. The officer felt it wise to discontinue the interview until after Tess had gained some strength, and most importantly, had seen her daughter.

The orderlies wheeled Tess's hospital bed to the children's ward where Rachel was spending her second night in hospital. Rachel smiled in her sleep while Tess rained kisses and caresses onto her sunburned features. This was such a comfort to Tess- though she soon sank back into her pillow and allowed herself to be wheeled back to her own room. She he did not have the energy to lean over to Rachel any longer. She grew weirdly aware as she rumbled back to her ward, that the squeaking of one of the wheels of the moving bed sent unpleasant shooting sensations across her skull. The lights overhead flitted and made her motion sick. Tess was mightily relieved to see Rachel but was exhausted by the effort and wincing in pain. She smiled gratefully when the orderly parked her bed and drew the curtains around her, although she was not free to seek slumber or pain relief right away, as she addressed the patient policewoman.

Unable to assist with the enquiries of the police, she felt keen frustration added to her other woes. Others would increasingly share her frustration in the long days ahead. Much to the disappointment of the rookie young officer who, whilst she did not let the veneer of professionalism slip, had been suppressing considerable excitement at being present when the victim regained consciousness. Tess however, recalled nothing. She was helpless to give any insight into who the driver of the other vehicle was. She was genuinely surprised that it hadn't been a single vehicle accident.

"You mean it wasn't my fault? Most things are," she had rasped feebly.

"No, ma'am. The preliminary report indicates that the driver of the other vehicle did not give way as he emerged from the lane. Mercifully, upon impact, you were driving well below the speed limit as indicated by the brake skid. What was your error however, Ma'am, was of course failing to use your seat belt, and eh… the reason you were flung from your vehicle. Your initial injuries are due to this breach of the law. Fortunately, your slow speed saved your life when you were propelled from your vehicle."

The officer paused as she considered the possible scenarios flitting through Tess's mind; her humanity wrestling with her professionalism.

"The other driver fled the scene," the officer continued, unable to remove the tone of disgust in her delivery. "Already at fault, the criminal culpability is compounded by fleeing the scene of an accident, let alone leaving an injured mother and child on scene to fend for themselves… well, maybe he had some heart - it appears that the offender placed an old blanket over you before leaving the scene to minimise shock… presumably. This is where we need your help, Tess, if any memories return … anything which might help us identify the other driver, please, please get a nurse to write your recollections down right away, if you can't. Call me. Here is my card. No doubt Sarge will look in on you too."

Before leaving, the officer explained how and where Tess had been found. Tess struggled, trying to digest all this information. So much to process, so many different thoughts and feelings bombarded her aching mind. She determined that she really must find a way to express her thanks to Tom and the rescue team when she could. She was concerned that Rachel had felt frightened enough to run away. She was frustrated that she was helpless to assist with any information about the other vehicle. The last thing she remembered was arranging eggs on the passenger seat of her Corolla. She knew that it was such a mercy, that on account of the egg delivery, she had been driving a lot slower than she normally would have been. However, the fact that the car had been t-boned by a driver who didn't give way and then who didn't stay long at the scene, outraged her. Tess conceded that at least some of the serious medical consequences she faced were of her own creation. She'd essentially neglected her own safety. No seatbelt had pinned Tess to the driver's seat when that car came out of nowhere. Typical of Tess, who was a heady mix of recklessness and maternal love.

Tess strained her mind, scrolling for important recollections. She increasingly became distressed and agitated. An alarm brashly *beeped,* indicating a dangerous spike in blood pressure and heart rate. The night nurse materialised almost instantly and paged the doctor on call. A sedative was given, and Tess slept with a slight smile, reassured again by her nurse as she closed her eyes that she at least had proof that Rachel was safe.

The next morning, no memories had returned. The ache and pressure inside Tess's head had not dissipated. Poor Tess could barely cope with even opening her eyes. It was decided as a matter of urgency by her medical team that she would be placed in an induced coma right away. It was hardly surprising, after the double trauma she had experienced that the scans which showed some highly worrying swelling on her brain. There was no luxury of time. Tess was in grave danger of death or permanent brain damage.

To be ejected through a windscreen head-first, and to later stumble down a blast hole, receiving a nasty additional head injury, all in one dramatic twenty-four period, was quite the talking-point around the bustling regional hospital.

"Geez … so lucky! That lady should buy a lotto ticket!" one orderly commented to another.

"She probably would if she didn't feel like the big red ball had been dropped on her head, mate," quipped the other.

"'Spose you would need to be awake anyway, to appreciate winning the big one."

# Rachel

1

Physically, Rachel bounced back from her ordeal reasonably quickly. It was extremely fortunate that she'd been found before dark and hadn't endured a night in the elements like her mother. In the ambulance she required a little oxygen and was understandably dazed and feverish - largely as result of the mumps virus still present in her diminutive system. She was monitored for forty-eight hours with the precaution of an intravenous line. Her little body welcomed the fluids which offset her dehydration and shock. She was administered regular paracetamol for her high temperature. All physical examinations revealed only scratches and scrapes consistent with hiding in the rocks and previous childish play. Her feet needed particular attention, because she had been barefoot in the bush. The only evidence that she'd been in a car accident, however, was the growing discoloration of her skin at the site where the seatbelt had tightened suddenly and did the job it was meant to. No bodily harm had befallen her from the offender.

Rachel missed the event of her first ever ambulance ride. She had awoken as she was wheeled under the glaring hospital lights as they rushed over her. Her eyes had widened as she struggled to take in her surroundings, but she closed her eyes again peacefully when she'd sighted Sarge. She'd submitted lethargically to a long and careful medical examination. Photographic evidence was gathered. Rachel could hear the pen scratching while lots of observations were scribbled down. Strangely, she did not fuss when the cannula was deftly inserted into her hand. The blur of regular intrusions and the beep of the thermometer in her ear barely seemed to register with her. There was a detailed process of inspecting and cleaning the many scratches and abrasions on her arms, legs and feet. A mixture of stoicism and shock kept what was normally a fidgety child, remarkably still. No chatter came from her lips. The only preference or concern she expressed was seen in her eyes, which continually searched for wherever Sarge was, in amongst all the happenings. When she grew a little agitated on occasion, her hand crept out from under the blanket and twisted a stray tendril of hair mechanically. She grew docile again when Sarge could position himself to hold her hand or sit where she could see him. It was no good him sitting by her as the doctors and nurses worked, she needed him to be in her line of sight, or to hold her hand.

She noticed him dab his moist eyes when she placed her small, tanned hand inside his great, pale paw. Safe. She liked how he joked with her, thanking her for the excuse to chaperone her ambulance and use the flashing lights on his police vehicle. He winked at her and told her that he'd held off on the siren except at intersections, because she wasn't that sick. Rachel would smile and nod on occasion but would only stare at him when he asked her a question directly about the accident, or after. Sarge stayed and stayed but knew that he couldn't be Rachel's security blanket all night. Rachel and he began to yawn. He didn't just want to slip out when she drifted off to sleep and risk her waking in distress to discover he had left her.

Once the flurry of test and note-taking had subsided, Sarge gently took the time to prepare Rachel for his departure. He explained to her that volunteers from their community were going to search for her mummy as soon as the sun woke-up in the morning. He chatted on and on about arrangements made with neighbours to feed the Moloney's animals, of how he would arrange for Anna to visit as soon as it was possible and many other soothing words. Even though it was a one-sided conversation, he gently reasoned with Rachel - he needed to go home to Anna who would be keen to know that her friend was doing fine. Much to the officer's relief, when it came time to leave, Rachel absorbed all his explanations with understanding and equanimity and even returned the policeman's wave when he left her ward. She tried to return his wink but was not able to coordinate it. She giggled at her failed effort. Policeman and child grinned at each other on parting.

Afterwards, two paediatric nurses took Rachel to a cavernous bath in a sterile, echoing room. They talked brightly yet softly to her, as she silently swirled the bubbles. They didn't use words like *accident* or *ordeal* but instead they chatted about how she'd been so brave on her big adventure at *Budgi,* cooing that she had done the right thing to take stranger-danger seriously and hide herself away until she recognised someone, she knew who was safe. Rachel had nodded solemnly as the nurses had spoken to her, seeming to accept the truth of what they said. Her eyes were deep pools of knowing and experience which belied her age as she, with the faintest of smiles, played with the yellow rubber duck which had been added to the glorious bubbles. Rachel was content to manoeuvre the bath toy in and around the foam for some time. She frowned at one point as she thought of her ducks at home. She would normally have fed them before nightfall and made sure that they were shut away for the night, safe in their pen, away from the crafty foxes.

It was ever so late when the two nurses sat Rachel down for supper at the small table and chairs next to her bed. Rachel pushed around the cold, congealed eggs on the plate. She pulled off the crusts of the soggy toast and nibbled a corner of the torn bread. Frowning, she cast it aside. It had margarine on it, a foreign substance to a little girl whose lineage traced generations of dairy farmers.

She pointed to the high bed, yawning. Asleep the instant they assisted her to climb in, Rachel was oblivious for the next eleven hours, despite observations taken intermittently as she slept.

2

Rachel Moloney's condition, as well as the dramatic context of her rescue, was occupying the thoughts of many at the hospital, including a savvy, young registrar in his first year of internship. Rostered for the drudgery of the late-early shift, it meant that he was on duty when Rachel was brought in on the night of her rescue, and that he also backed up for the morning shift after his five hours rest. He was on hand when the child woke after a much longer slumber. Fuelled by caffeine and interest, the registrar was sharp and thorough in reviewing Rachel Moloney's chart of observations, and in making his own. His little patient had yet to utter a word. Rachel wouldn't be drawn on any question posed to her.

He scribbled *traumatic mutism* on his chart with a question mark. This condition had been a study of his for one of his numerous medical assignments whilst training, but this would be his first live case in a hospital placement. It had been noted again and again that the child had not engaged verbally with rescuers or medics. The doctor had spoken to the bulky policeman who'd accompanied Rachel into Accident and Emergency. He took the time to obtain as many details as he could about what Rachel had endured in the last twenty-four hours - not that the hospital staff were talking about much else, when at that time her mother had yet to be located, to top off the whole drama.

91

*Weird business,* he thought.

He had witnessed an unmistakable bond between policeman and child. It was the doctor's understanding that while Rachel obviously trusted the familiar face of her local policeman when she was retrieved from under the rocky overhang, she was not forthcoming about her experience. The Sergeant had waited patiently at the hospital for some time, hopeful to catch a moment when the child's tongue was loosened. He was wise not to stay overnight, however, for this fruitless cause. The officer had returned to his family after a massive day when it became evident that the child would give nothing away and wouldn't be distressed by his leaving. The staff and were all briefed not to ask Rachel too many questions but to alert the police if something was to be disclosed. A young female constable took over the vigil, discreetly placed in the hallway, in case the child did reveal information.

*Mmmmm... Unusual, but understandable,* mused the overworked doctor. It was more likely for a toddler to possibly experience a temporary setback in language development after such an ordeal, but there were some cases of older children who stopped talking if they felt threatened or traumatised.

3

Rachel was delighted when on Wednesday afternoon, Anna arrived for a visit with Sarge. She was feeling so much better now the fever had subsided. The pair huddled together in the high, narrow bed and Anna read to her friend some stories she'd borrowed from the book-corner from school. The policeman sat patiently. Rachel liked the policeman just being there. She would occasionally look over and smile.

His mission at that point in time was just to be a part of the furniture. Just Anna's dad. His presence needed to seem normal to a child who had undergone a traumatic experience. He had to continue to be non-threatening.

Sarge asked the young doctor on his evening rounds what he thought about Rachel's lack of verbal communication. The registrar explained that paediatrics wasn't really his area of expertise, nor psychology. He suggested that stressful situations surrounding accidents or trauma could trigger an unwillingness to talk and it was unclear what would prompt Rachel to speak, but perhaps she might speak to another child instead of an adult, especially one in authority. The earnest intern sympathised with Sarge, but this was not of any assistance to a waiting police investigation. Sarge intimated that even if Rachel did speak to Anna about the accident (which at this stage hadn't been observed), clearly, witness testimony couldn't be given on behalf of a vicarious playmate.

The doctor nodded, grasping how Rachel's silence complicated the police investigation. He could only offer what would be obvious to even the medically untrained - Rachel was likely having trouble processing, let alone communicating about what had happened in the last twenty-four hours. He directed Sarge to his case notes:

*Consultation with a Child Psychologist, highly recommended. Referral to be supplied. In-patient care should be considered.*

Sarge had plenty of time to digest this information as he sat in the vinyl armchair by Rachel Moloney's bed. He observed what a tight unit his daughter and Rachel were - happy to be together. Rachel seemed unconcerned that mum was not on hand, reclining against a stack of starched pillows on her hospital bed with the sides up. Anna wedged herself at the side of her best friend. She proudly read a glossy book she had packed. It was really a book for much younger kids, but they liked all the little illustrations and funny labels for different kinds of transport. Sarge appeared to be mesmerised by the storytelling, as well.

At a suitable interval, Sarge lent forward and gently asked Rachel if she remembered anything about the driver of the other car in the accident she'd been in. Did the car look like any in the storybook? His police notepad was ready on his lap. Rachel's eyes misted over but she said nothing.

Later, when the little girls were returning from a trip to the bathroom, giggling and pushing the intravenous trolley between them, they stopped in front of the afternoon-tea cart parked in the doorway to the children's ward. Sarge had a clear line of sight and was in good hearing distance to witness Rachel stop abruptly and tug on Anna's hand. Anna then stepped forward and spoke to the kitchen staffer, Rachel nodding like a puppet all the while.

"We would like a biscuit, please," Anna announced with her most charming of smiles. Rachel, through mute signing, clearly indicated both her choice of cookie and her appreciation. The two looked at each other.

"Thank you. We really like your pink apron and hat, too," said Anna.

Rachel had no need of speech when she had Anna to speak for her.

They were still together, the girls wiping crumbs off the hospital sheets, when the earnest young policewoman knocked on the door and came in beaming brightly.

"Rachel! Your mum has been found at last!"

Rachel's eyes were enormous as the details of the double-edged, extraordinary tale were imparted to her. The young officer focused on the good news of her mother's rescue-being located in such an extraordinary manner, and that she was getting the best medical attention. Hopefully Rachel could see her mother when she regained consciousness.

"It's like something you'd read in a book," pronounced Anna.

All present nodded in agreement. Normally Rachel would have chimed in. Not so now. Rachel remained silent.

Perhaps Rachel didn't really grasp at that point the danger that Tess was in and was happy knowing that Tess was no longer lying cold, hurt and alone. The ICU was the Intensive Care Unit - and she really wanted her mum to have lots of care after her ordeal.

4

Thursday morning brought news that Tess had woken up for a few hours in the night and had been in to kiss Rachel. Rachel touched her face at the place where the kisses landed. She smiled when she was told how her mum had held her hand on her own and rejoiced that Rachel was safe.

Her smile did not linger when she was then informed that this morning had brought with it a distinct deterioration in Tess's condition. It was carefully explained to Rachel how serious her mother's condition was. Anna, who had come for a short visit before settling back into her normal school routine, held Rachel's hand tightly. The registrar did his best. Inducing a coma decreases the brain's electrical activity and metabolic rate, so the doctor explained to Rachel that putting her mother to sleep allowed her brain to rest. He was at pains to say that Tess was being well looked after, but this was the best way to protect Tess's brain from further injury.

The two friends listened intently, nodding that they understood. There was one moment of alarm however, when Anna volunteered a question - hadn't Rachel's puppy Benjie, been *put to sleep* after biting Rachel? He'd never come home again. The doctor, seeing his mistake, hurriedly assured the children that Tess could and would be woken up again. Rachel switched from staring first at Anna and then at the doctor, with furtive glances at Sarge in the background.

Rachel rubbed her eyes; there was much to absorb. She'd been told that Tess had regained consciousness and briefly visited her in the early hours of the morning, when she was sound asleep. Yet before another visit could be arranged in daylight hours when Rachel was awake, Tess's condition had taken a dramatic turn for the worse and she'd been placed in an induced coma. Ironically, Rachel and Tess kept missing each other like characters in a modern-day Shakespearean tragedy.

Sarge had made a seemingly casual visit, bringing his daughter with him, secretly hoping that Rachel would be ready to answer the questions that really needed to be answered on the third day after the crime had been committed. How long could he wait for Rachel to provide the breakthrough the police needed into their inquiry into the hit and run incident? Eight-year-old Rachel was proving a reluctant witness. The matter would take some delicacy. Any efforts to coax testimony from the only eye- witness he had at his disposal were hampered by Tess's worsening situation, rightfully drawing away the spotlight.

The growing team of people connected with Rachel's situation had a roundtable meeting later that morning. In attendance were medical staff, police, and now a social worker who had been assigned to oversee the wellbeing of the child with no parent able to care for her. Rachel was no longer just an individual; she had become a case file. It was unanimously decided that Rachel couldn't be released from care yet. The child had almost made a full recovery physically but would remain in hospital or some other care unit, until it was decided what the best next step was. Her silence was unnerving, especially for those who'd known the normally chatty and effervescent child previously. The team also weighed up the reasons for and against Rachel visiting her mother and witnessing her so ill and unresponsive.

It was deemed important that Rachel see Tess, even if it was confronting. How else could the child grasp what was happening to her mother otherwise?

As a result, at the end of the third day since they had set out innocently to deliver some eggs, Rachel stood intently looking through the sterile glass of the intensive care unit. She gazed at her pretty mother - her repose summoning images of the fabled Sleeping Beauty from her bedtime stories. She said nothing. Her hand crept up and touched the glass for some moments and then settled back on the hair tucked behind her left ear. Nervously, she began to twist a wayward tendril over and over again.

# the Policeman and the Psychologist

## 1

Back at the station, Sarge sat weighing up the situation, reclining on his creaking office chair. While Sarge has received initial resources, and of course, assistance from the forensics team, it was clear that the case wasn't thought important enough for an Albury detective to be assigned. Now that mother and daughter had been retrieved, it was up to Sarge to solve the case by locating the offender. He didn't feel insulted in the least that the matter hadn't flagged more interest, up the chain of command.

*Sensible to leave the matter with the local copper,* thought Sarge.

He knew the district well and would be well placed if the culprit responsible for the hit-and-run was indeed a Table Top resident. People would surely notice a damaged vehicle, or indeed an injured party ... and all the community was talking about the event ... surely the crime couldn't be covered up indefinitely?

*Why won't she speak up?* Sarge almost said out loud. Rachel had evidently retreated to the safety of silence, but for what reason? Trauma? Fear? Threats?

*Maybe all the above?*

Weighing it all up, he reckoned that he had a reasonable trust connection with his small but silent star witness. Obviously, Rachel would be most comfortable in her own home and back in her school routine, with Anna at her side. Yet, if they were together, he could see that there was no incentive for Rachel to start speaking again, even about mundane things. Anna was an intuitive and effective mouthpiece for her friend.

Rachel would not be drawn to answer any questions about the accident, whenever or however he subtly tried to draw her out. While the case had been deemed best left in local hands (meaning it was all up to him on the ground) the Albury chief detective had reiterated his penchant for procedure, in no uncertain terms. As a result, Sarge had ensured that all the medics were briefed that it was vital to treat the child routinely. She was not to be questioned about what had happened, outside of an official capacity. This was standard procedure to preserve the admissibility of any evidence provided by a child witness. Naturally, kids were suggestible. Evidence obtained from children could be easily torn apart under cross-examination, if there was any hint of manipulation, and at best, could be construed as unreliable.

He and the court-assigned female child advocate formed the official capacity. Sending additional detectives in, who didn't have the established trust that Sarge had with the witness, would be counter-productive at this point in proceedings. District Office had offered to send through some tips for dealing with victims and witnesses who were children.

Sarge pulled the supposedly helpful suggestions off the fax machine. Scratching his stubbled chin, he read with a frown of concentration:

Helpful Hints for Relating to Child Witnesses.

1.  Get down on the child's level. Sit on the floor and play with them.

    *Struth. Common sense, 'specially for a cop who's also the father of a*

2.  Notice (and chat about) the smallest of things: a piece of fluff on the carpet, a spot on the wall, the wind of the spinning fan, and the ants on the ground.

    *Okay…*

3.  Get excited about ordinary things, like rubbish being removed by the garbage truck.

    *Thanks experts … we don't even have kerbside bin service in Table Top.*

4.  Don't talk too much, try communicating with as few words as possible.

*Now that was more his style. Yep. Rachel would probably relate to that. She'd nailed this strategy herself!*

Sarge's rueful cynicism to lighten the seriousness of the situation, wasn't sustainable. He grasped all too well the grim facts. Essentially, he was dealing with a voluntarily non-verbal child witness. Expert help, which extended beyond this so-called (but not so helpful) facsimile *factsheet;* his personal experience of relating to children; and his police training, - was clearly all going be required. Most importantly, it could well be imperative for the child's long-term well-being.

Sarge knew that finding a suitable child psychologist full-stop, let alone one who was willing to work with a kid, plus Child Services *and* police - in the country, was not going to be easy. He made a terse call to District HQ and then a more relational call to Social Services. He recognised that the child could need ongoing counselling, if she was ever going to be able to give evidence. Rachel would need to find her voice for her own benefit, not just for the reason of solving his case.

A day later than Sarge would've liked, the name and phone extension of Dr Christina King, of *Desmond House,* Wentworth Street, Manly, was given to him. A phone appointment was quickly set up by a very helpful receptionist, who grasped that a traumatised child needed attention; a far cry from the complications created by his superiors and the casual attitude he had encountered by professionals in his local area. Frustratingly, evidence was going cold while he played bureaucratic table-tennis and worked the phones.

The Doctor of Child Psychology had been provided with updated hospital notes and reports from the various agencies who were now dealing with the Rachel Moloney case. Dr King would study them before the agreed upon phone appointment, so she could advise him on how to proceed with the interview of Rachel.

Interestingly, the social worker had advised Sarge that Rachel's family situation was already on the welfare radar and the child labelled as 'at-risk' even before the current unique crisis had emerged. Was it any wonder that the child was allowing others to translate her? Rachel, already labelled and now assigned a case number, had traded in her power of voice.

*Hope you can help us out, Doc!*

Sarge willed it to be so, as he whispered this plea in his head. Nancy patched the call through from just a few meters away. Formalities were observed in this country station, on occasion, when appropriate. He could hear her dial the extension using her pen to pull back each number.

After the obligatory greetings and preliminaries were covered, the policeman and psychologist delved into the complexities of the matter. Doctor Christina King gave her initial, expert view in low confident tones, as she endeavoured to paint the backdrop, against which the hit-and-run event had occurred.

"Every individual and indeed, all parents, operate with an element of dysfunction. All of us sit somewhere on the continuum of functionality and dysfunction - everyone. So, there is no judgement when I say that parents struggle with functioning well in all areas of life, all the time." She paused to allow her listener to absorb the foundation she was laying.

"Teenage Mums, policemen, psychologists included… every parent… all have areas of dysfunction," she emphasised.

"My wife would endorse your assessment. I'm not married to the job, but I reckon Sarah would agree that I don't always function in a way she finds helpful," he offered ruefully.

"Right."

Sarge could discern the smile in her voice, even over the phone.

"All relationships and families have strengths and weaknesses. However, children from…em…dysfunctional environments, who experience trauma as a part of their formative experience, officer, are bound to default to certain self-protection settings. Now, again, when I say *dysfunction,* I mean no disrespect to the mother," reassured the voice at the other end of the line. "I understand that Tess Moloney is fighting for her life and when she pulls through, it is always the goal of child services to support whole families, rather than separate them indefinitely."

Sarge indicated his agreement over the phone.

"Child Services has provided me with their paperwork, indicating that this family was known to them before the accident," the psychologist continued. "Let's see… yes, there were a couple of calls from a preschool teacher citing low-level neglect. The matter was investigated, but no action was required to be taken. There were some potentially concerning observations made by staff… and minor disclosures, innocently made by the little girl herself, which were caused the commencement of a case file."

"What kind of matters and disclosures?" Sarge questioned.

"Things like Rachel repeatedly being brought late to educational programs. Hmm… let me see, what else… Rachel arrived very sleepy to sessions after apparently not being put to bed during a few all-night parties… and, oh yes, it was documented that Rachel had mentioned that it was hard to wake her mum in the mornings and that she'd scrounge for food, preparing her own breakfasts, or even lunch. There was suspicion of excessive alcohol use in the home, maybe even illegal drugs? Nothing was proven, the case was put to bed, but child services kept everything on file. The notes did also include other indications that Tess loved and cared for Rachel, overall."

Sarge interjected, "I did get the feeling that relocating to our small community was Tess turning over a new leaf. Look, Rachel has more freedom than some, but she relishes living in our tiny town."

"Yes. From what I understand, Tess Moloney… reading between the lines, has made a heroic effort in keeping her child in the first place. Teenage motherhood is a tough gig, full stop. It would have been perfectly understandable if Tess had given her child up for adoption … or required help from the foster-care system once her marriage was dissolved. Tess chose to love and raise Rachel herself, in what must've been immensely challenging circumstances."

"True that." In Sarge's mind, Tess possessed some good instincts when it came to looking after her little one. Yet on other occasions, he could be left scratching his head in astonishment… like regarding her blatant disregard for her own personal safety, for example. This had ultimately contributed to the vulnerable situation her little family was in currently. As such a young mum, she didn't always succeed at rising above the hubris of youth. Teenagers and young adults often thought that (or acted like) the laws of the land, or even the laws of physics, just didn't apply to them. "It's heartbreaking that a woman in her early twenties is in a coma as we speak, because she disregarded the law of motion or thought that she was invincible. She knew enough to strap-in her child, mercifully," he said.

"Yes, children may live in a household which has much love but can nonetheless remain subject to the whims of a struggling, inconsistent or even irresponsible carer. Needs must, the kids in such homes learn to adapt accordingly, for their own self-preservation. For their own safety, such children develop a working rulebook, if I can phrase it like that - which makes sense to them."

"Well, talking of rules, Rachel isn't always known to follow the school rules, even though she loves going to school. What sorts of things are you referring to, Doc?"

"Right. Circumstances teach kids to be very wary. They astutely glean from different life experiences that they must look out for themselves and to conduct themselves in certain ways if they are to be safe. All households have rules, but 'at risk' children quickly internalise messages which then become mantras to live by. Things like:

*You didn't see what you saw*, or

*You didn't hear what you heard*, and above all,

*Don't talk about what you didn't see and didn't hear.*

The policeman expelled a long, low sound in response.

"Dysfunctional right? Yet such rules are often communicated and reinforced in even the most loving but flawed families. These rules become internalised and combined with the self-preservation instincts of children who we might suggest have very real reasons to be fearful, can become a difficult fortress to penetrate."

"It's smart to protect yourself, I guess," offered Sarge.

"You can't really argue with that logic," agreed the doctor.

Sarge continued, "I understand that Rach is bright. I reckon she's had to be savvy enough to navigate, some ... ah, tricky situations. Let's face it, Tess, God love her, has virtually had to grow up at the same time as her kid. She was still a child herself when she found out she was gonna be a parent."

Together the policeman and the psychologist exchanged their understanding of the case of Rachel Moloney and developed a plan of action. By the close of business, they had liaised with Child Services, Albury Police and the hospital. They arranged to bring Rachel to Desmond House the next day if her hospital discharge went ahead as scheduled at the registrar's 7:00 A.M rounds.

"Nancy!" he barked, "Please book three tickets on the mail train to Sydney tomorrow and confirm this with Social Services. Oh, and please fax the final recommendation from the psych through to Liza Egan, Child Advocate."

# Part 2

# Rachel

1

An eager pixie face looked out of the smeared carriage window with great interest. Rachel couldn't recall ever going on a train before. She remembered looking at a photo of herself in her mother's arms on an airstrip. Perhaps she had boarded a train to get to the airport as that tiny baby on that day? She feels both excited and anxious to take it all in. Her eyes darted to and fro with so much to look at. She felt a little dizzy.

It had been carefully explained to Rachel that while her mother was asleep for medical reasons, she was going to go for a little holiday to the city where she'd get to meet someone who could help her with how she was feeling after the accident. She'd stared blankly at the kind but distant adult who had informed her of this. There'd been so many grown-ups trying to make friends with her, all with lots of questions that she'd been unable, or unwilling to answer.

Rachel watched the towns slip by, growing increasingly catatonic as she stared at the blurring landscape. Involuntarily, she slipped her fingers into the side of her fine hair, rhythmically twirling it in sync with the movement of the train. She resisted the urge to put her thumb in her mouth, she was much too old for that!Out of the corner of her eye she noticed that her minders seemed to be getting equally sleepy. The monotony of the countryside rushing by as the train built up speed after each station stop, had a calming,

almost hypnotic effect on all of them. Liza, her assigned female social worker
- normally chatty and social in all senses of the word, was lulled into silence.
Rachel noticed that even so, she kept a careful eye on her charge. Eventually,
Rachel pulled away reluctantly from the scenes outside the window. She
struggled to keep her eyes open. Valiantly she snapped her head back again.
Dimly she was aware of Sarge grumbling, "This ruddy train trip is slow as a
wet week," before she lost her fight with sleep.

Rachel kept slipping off the leather seat when the train jerked to a stop at
the platforms. Sarge and Liza scrambled to catch her. If the little girl didn't
look so fragile, it would have almost been humorous to watch. Sensibly, Liza
intervened before it could happen too often, and she laid Rachel down gently
on the floor, providing her own coat to line the narrow strip of floor, making
a bed of sorts for the little girl.

"Not an entirely unwelcome opportunity to think and for Rachel to
rest," Sarge murmured dryly.

Rachel was no longer fidgeting. Instead, the train rocked and soothed.
Even the adults in the compartment indulged in some sneaky shuteye as the
snail mail train crept to Sydney.

2

When they arrived at the pandemonium of Central Station, they all felt
refreshed, and were relieved to stretch their cramped legs. Scooting out of the
way of the blur of suits darting in every direction took all their concentrated
efforts. Liza suggested that they walk down to Circular Quay, with the view
to board the next ferry to Manly.

Rachel assented with an enthusiastic nod of her head when Liza asked if
she'd like to stroll down to the harbour, rather than catch a taxi. Sarge easily

shouldered the bags, with Liza pulling her own compact overnight case on wheels. She was clearly the most experienced traveller of the three and Sarge was content to let Liza lead the way.

"This is my turf," she declared.

Liza studied at Sydney Uni, and of course had taken this same journey with several vulnerable or disadvantaged country kids well before Rachel was added to her caseload.

They all thoroughly enjoyed the walk. Rachel trotted along, her eyes sparkling as she took in the glittering cityscape. She seemed energised by this new environment and embraced the fresh adventure. She wasn't intimidated by the imposing structures around her, but with her head high, Rachel keenly inhaled every experience in her diminutive sights.

Sarge marvelled at the resilience of the kid as he looked at Rachel with a grin, appreciative of her infectious excitement. This trip was likely a welcome distraction from recent events, he reflected. Sarge's concerns about taking this previously uncharted course of action in his working life were assuaged somewhat by the interest and enjoyment the child showed in her surroundings.

It was as if Rachel was waking up from the walking-slumber she'd been in. Tess may have been in an actual coma, but Rachel herself had functioned in a dream-like state, when not distracted by Anna. Sarge observed that the Rachel he'd interacted with prior to her trauma, was beginning to surface again. She wasn't yet speaking words, but Sarge had a good feeling about where things were heading. Surely putting distance between her and Table Top would have to be helpful in making her feel safe?

They weaved their way through Circular Quay to Wharf Three, where they'd board the next ferry bound for Manly. There was no need to stress or to bother with timetables, as Liza pointed out, the ferries ran every thirty minutes. Rachel exhibited all the signs of excitement a little girl possibly could, without audibly chattering. Her eyes darted everywhere at once, she hopped from one leg to another while waiting in the queue and skipping along the pier and then the gang plan with the broadest grin on her face.

It certainly was a magnificent afternoon on the quay, full of the sparkle and light, which the artist, Arthur Streeton, a generation previous, had loved to paint into his renowned works, also inspired by Sydney Harbour. Sometimes visitors to the city found the foreshore miserably damp, with sea and sky a dull grey, but not on this occasion. Glorious Sydney! A shimmering, living landscape on exhibition for even the most artistically ignorant to appreciate.

Rachel tilted her chin to the breeze and the warm sunshine. Her mouth fell open in awe as she watched the famous 'Coathanger' (Harbour Bridge) come into full view as they glided by.

Pulling into Manly Harbour was wonderful too, with its pretty round pier and the white arches of beach buildings slowly growing larger and larger. Behind the buildings were lines of giant pines, with red-roofed houses peeking through the branches and more modest flats facing the sea on the hills behind. The endless deep blue of the sky above was superimposed with clouds so fluffy and like white cotton balls, that Rachel thought they looked like they could have just been glued on, like in one of her craft activities.

Sarge thought it all simply breathtaking. Small ocean craft bobbed cheerfully at their moorings in the foreground of the vista before them. He suddenly had an urge to go fishing, and be free of cares and commitments, in this charming cove.

Liza smiled to herself as she remembered long summer days in her late teens, spent shrieking and splashing friends in the fenced tidal pool, alternating with long, drowsy stretches of irresponsibly sunning themselves.

Two very different off-siders than those of her university days, disembarked the ferry with Liza at Manly wharf. Wading through the crush of people, Liza clutched the silent child's hand, while Sarge hovered protectively on the other side of Rachel. Flanking the child, they navigated around the bursting bicycle racks and over the pedestrian crossing, carefully traversing the hectic East Esplanade. They automatically lingered under the shade of the gnarled Moreton Bay Figs to orient themselves and enjoy the stately shade. Their gaze lifted to a gorgeous old antebellum style building, resplendent with white shutters and six two-story columns marking the portico at its entrance. People sat on the well-kept grass or park benches eating enticing looking ice-creams.

"Lotsa people take the ferry over here just so they can choose an ice-cream at this shop, so they must taste alright," Sarge said in his slow, conversational way, pointing out an iconic ice-cream parlour as they started to stroll up the street again

"What's your favourite flavoured ice-cream Rachel?" wheedled Liza, "Tell me."

The small girl looked back at her unblinking and merely shrugged.

"Well, we should have some free time at some stage, if you want to come back here. What do you think?"

Rachel looked past the social worker with an inscrutable glint in her eye.

*What kid doesn't take the bait of ice-cream?* the police officer thought ruefully.

*Kids know when you're trying too hard though. 'Specially this one.*

Rachel did linger a little however, looking past the queue into the display cases of the advertised forty flavours.

They took their time strolling up the Manly Corso, so as not to bump into the crowds of sightseers and backpackers. This was no hardship when Sydney had presented them with such a sparkling summer evening. There were loads of young people chatting and laughing outside of the Backpackers Lodge and happy hour seemed to be well underway, as Sarge steered Rachel past the hilarity escaping the various hotel balconies. Everywhere was bird song, competing with the human merriment. The array of figs and palms as they meandered along the Corso, housed hundreds of squawking birds. Running diagonally off the main mall were intriguing little lanes and cobbled thoroughfares. Rachel secretly hoped that there would be time for exploring new haunts. She simply loved to explore!

The giant Norfolk pines loomed ahead as they came closer to Steyne Street. A low brick wall was all that separated the walkways from the beach. Like true north on a compass, the pines seemed to draw the crowds being funnelled through the mall to the other side of the Point, with yet another dazzling sweep of ocean vistas. What a place! Manly Cove and the harbour behind them, Manly Beach ahead and the charms of gracious old-world architecture in between.

Carefully crossing the busy roadway, looking both ways as instructed by the words and arrows painted on the road, they stood under the long curve of Norfolk pines. Rachel craned her neck and gazed at the height and splendour of this well- loved landmark. Instead of intimidating her, the soaring trees beckoned invitingly to the little girl. Unmoving, with eyes glued to the century old trees she inhaled deeply, marvelling at the salty edge to the air. These pine sentinels comfortably remind her of her own adopted lunchtime pine tree at Table Top Central School.

Liza Egan stooped down so she could match Rachel's eye level, mistaking the child's faltering steps and deep breathing as an indication that her charge was struggling with a new location so far from home. Rachel tolerated this virtually unknown lady who smelled of musk, with kind eyes wrinkled at the sides. Liza chattered softly but with bright tones about the beach and the rocks to be explored just around the Point, wanting to soothe any of Rachel's assumed nervousness.

Rachel smiled to herself.

*I love climbing and exploring on rocks.*

Indeed, she did love clambering over the rocks of her hill. A shutter closed quickly over her countenance, like a cloud eclipsing the sunlight that had shone only seconds before.

Liza looked gently brushes the child's cheek as she rose to her feet. "There's a lot going on behind those eyes," she muttered to Sarge, as they continued.

All three basked in the sunlit beachside walk, pausing often so Rachel could look out into the vast ocean. A stillness, even greater than her lack of conversation, came over the child. She lost herself, staring into the boundless horizon - a creeping calm created by the distance between Rachel's ordeal and the present. Adult-like concerns and stresses had been weighing heavily on Rachel, succeeding to mummify a previously chatty and carefree child. Fresh sights and sounds were already weaving their magic on the child, wrapped in her own thoughts and torment.

Rachel felt lighter, but not free.

Surreptitiously, she studied her case worker. She noticed how relaxed Liza was - obviously loving the seascape. Sarge was also grinning appreciatively at the vista. Standing tall, with his shoulders back. A twitch next to his left eye belied his impatience; his relaxation was more an assumed pose of disciplined stillness. Their destination was only meters away.

Finally, Rachel and her minders rounded Wentworth Street and accessed the side entrance of a large facility, which sprawled over a huge corner block with the beach only just across the road. After the shortest of walks, they halted. The brass plate fixed to the brick work gleamed in the late afternoon light, showcasing Desmond House. Rachel looked up and up, attempting to take in the imposing five-storey building towering over her at street level. Sarge stepped in behind her, fearing his charge would topple backwards. Liza found the cast iron doorknocker and rapped it twice smartly. It heralded a most satisfying announcement of their arrival.

# Sarge and the Psychologist

1

Sarge noted that this was the smarter side of the facility, boasting ambient and well-maintained offices and meeting rooms. The main building and adjacent quadrangle, which he had caught a glimpse of over the fence before they had rounded the corner, were not so pleasant (other than having a sweeping view of the beach -which certainly counted for something). Built with unfortunate drab bricks and cement, the main buildings housed the children's dormitories, a dining room, school, and recreation areas which were more reminiscent of a prison - at best an orphanage, than the upmarket medical clinic they were soon ushered into.

As a nuanced facility, Desmond House boasted short-term accommodation for children and their parents or carers. Therapy took a day or two and involved multiple sessions. These intensives were a relatively new phenomenon that proved not just to be practical for out-of-town clients but effective as well. Sessions were varied according to the age of the child and the therapy required.

Short notice meant that while they'd successfully obtained rooms on site, there was only a limited number of contact appointments with Doctor Christina King available. Earlier on the telephone, the doctor had explained to the police officer that he and the accompanying social worker would need to consider recreational outings and mealtimes as kind of an 'accidental therapy' and of course, potentially, a natural interviewing opportunity, when the child-witness found her voice. King had explained that when Rachel broke her silence, it could well occur in a non-formal setting. Obviously, a child might feel less comfortable volunteering information in a formal therapy context or understandably, in strict police questioning settings.

Christina King's words were etched in Sarge's mind after the phone consultation the day previous- "Make no mistake, Sergeant, I know this may seem counterintuitive for you but your role at this point isn't really to conduct an interview." Dr King had paused to allow the constable to absorb what she was saying. "Actually, it's Rachel who'll be 'interviewing' you and the other authority figures and caregivers who've suddenly popped-up in her life. Including me. She won't need spoken language for this, but she'll be watching and listening bigtime! Hopefully, when she's relaxed, and if you and… ah, me… continue to pass her *trust test,* it's then that Rachel might become comfortable enough to communicate verbally."

2

Sarge left the child and case worker to settle into the colourful short-stay room. They were happily playing a game of scrabble. He thought if their focus was anything to go by, both adult and child were nerdy or competitive, or both.

He sank down into a plush armchair in the panelled waiting room outside the psychologist's office. After their phone consult, he'd arranged to meet with the resident expert, in person, in preparation for Rachel's first session.

Perusing a pamphlet on a low table beside him, Sarge read that Desmond House offered both outpatient and inpatient services, though the children who used the facility were called *guests* not *patients*. The mission statement of the centre indicated that it existed for the benefit of children from rural and remote areas - specialising in supporting vulnerable children.

*Situated at the heart of Sydney, only 7kms from Taronga Zoo, 9kms from Luna Park, Opera House and the Harbour Bridge, Desmond House enjoys a prime location to give country kids a wonderful time in Sydney while they access medical specialists.*

*Ha!* He thought wryly, Sydneysiders considered anywhere south of the Great Dividing Range as far-flung and too great a distance to travel.

It seemed that in addition to providing access to medical or psychological services, the goal of Desmond House was to give regional children both a city and beach experience, which they'd likely never experienced before. The policeman read with interest that the charity had existed since 1924 and was one of Australia's oldest, helping country kids access the healthcare they needed, no matter where they lived. The idea was birthed by a sickly reverend from central-west New South Wales, who'd recuperated from illness on a much-loved stay at Manly beach. Day after day of enjoying the temperate sea breeze and the tang of salt air had done wonders for him. The story captured Sarge's imagination, as did many an Aussie tale where the cause of the underdog was championed.

The brochure featured a photograph of a kindly man of the cloth with a beloved black Labrador seated democratically on a striped deck chair next to him. Newly invigorated, the church minister had committed himself to create this opportunity for convalescent children from remote or rural areas. Apparently, his vision of bringing country kids to the beach for respite, quickly became a reality in 1926. A local Manly doctor became aware of what was in his generation, a veritable wasteland of medical and social needs for country kids who lacked access to vital services. He began offering his consultations free of charge. The service grew. Just under one hundred kids attended the first seaside camp, but the summer-stay program continued for fifty years.

*Our feet in the sand and our hearts in the bush,* the promotional rhapsodised.

The Wentworth Street wing of the complex, where the policeman sat presently, was first used as a training centre for the nurses who would later staff the adjacent facility. The site then morphed into an iconic guest house where the matron worked to create a home away-from-home for country children coming for day appointments or longer treatments. Desmond House was officially opened in 1935. Then, in 1938 a primary school opened on site as well. Child patients who stayed for weeks rather than days wouldn't miss out on an education as teachers were supplied by the NSW Department of Education.

Tossing the glossy material back on the side table, the police officer straightened his tie and brushed a speck off his polished boot as he settled into thought. Sarge had been warned that Rachel might need to stay on for supervision at Desmond House after the intensive program, so a small but fully-fledged school on site for the benefit of long-stay children was handy.

*Might be best until Tess is fit for duty.*

He surmised that Rachel's domestic situation had been patchy in her early years, yet now, coupled with her mum out of action and with the way Rachel had retreated into herself, there was no other way to think about her, other than as *vulnerable.* It was sad, but true. He looked up at the framed cross-stitched sampler on the peach-coloured wall:

*Let the Little Children Come to Me,* it read.

The text was surrounded by rows of paper dolls, tulips and Victorian profiles which created a charming and effective border around the stitched lettering.

"Well, we've come! Good luck Doc, with getting her to open her mouth," he muttered ruefully.

He picked up the brochure again, reading that the facility also boasted numerous social workers and paediatric clinicians to help children with speech and language delays, behavioural and learning difficulties, and mental illness. He learned with interest that the outbreak of childhood polio in the 1940s meant that the facility developed an in-house splint and surgical boot-making department to meet the wave of need.

Sarge shuddered and counted his blessing that his own daughter had been spared any such terrible childhood illness, and that she was of the generation who received the polio vaccine. A few bitter drops on the tongues of boys and girls, lined up with their mouths gaping like baby birds while nurses with beaked caps efficiently tended to the young. Anna had grimaced along with her classmates at the taste of the foul medicine, but she'd obediently swallowed the vaccine. It seemed a small price to pay to eradicate a virus for the next generation - one which caused paralysis of limbs, deformity, or even death,

Sarge continued reading. The writer had left no promotional stone unturned, stating that after a visit from Queen Elizabeth II and Princess Anne, Desmond House was granted the possibility of attaching the official prefix 'Royal' in front of the name of their fine institution. There were obligatory black and white photographs of Her Royal Highness, bending down with gloved hand to accept a delicate posy from a shy but earnest little girl, wearing the then uniform of the children's home. Other dear little faces (some hopeful, some anxious) looked on, holding their small bunches of flowers expectantly. Some of the adult crowd looked a mangy lot, squinting into the bright sun or sporting outrageous sunglasses. The Queen herself, a long way from home, looked serene and gracious and was of course, wearing one of her signature matching hat and purse ensembles.

Sarge inspected the abundance of other glossy photographs teeming with bright eyed children in quaint uniforms against spectacular ocean backdrops. Interspersed amongst the subjects was the occasional child with an eye-patch or with an arm in a sling. Along with the watchful starched nurses and commanding matron, these were the only reminders that Desmond House was a health facility first and not strictly a holiday program. There were other more recent coloured pictures featuring children at play with festive kites on windy beaches, kicking up their heels in the sand.

Sarge felt relieved that the decision had been made to bring Rachel Moloney to this fine facility. She'd already perked up and appeared to be enjoying this new adventure. However, he did reflect that it might be a wise move for the place to leave off referring to the place as a *children's home*. He'd certainly be downplaying that terminology with his tiny charge. He certainly didn't want the kid to think they were sticking her in an orphanage (even temporarily). Or worse still, sow the seed that they'd given up on Tess ever getting better. Granted, it wasn't ideal that Rachel had been removed from her home life and would now be staying in a strange setting for as long as it took for her to be well and to speak again … or, at least until Tess was back on her feet (*if* she recovered). Which would happen first?

The policeman sighed to himself - there were a lot of variables to contend with, whichever way he looked at it; all out of his control. The reality was that Rachel's routine was rudely interrupted last week when she and her mum had innocently set out for a drive. Nothing was the same for Tess or Rachel since the moment of that fateful accident. It remained that he had a case to solve and a duty of care, which combined, had jolted him and taken him out of the sleepy rhythm of his life at Table Top. It was all a waiting game. Yet he preferred action.

The intensity of the past few days revisited the policeman as a wave of weariness. He stifled an unexpectedly loud yawn, looking around him apologetically. Attending the scene of the accident, the coordination of the search and rescue of the missing mother and daughter, the hospital visits and of course, all the extra administration attached to locating supports and resources needed for a child victim of crime, added up to a lot. He was used to a more laid-back pace of life in his regular duties. Lately, he'd not been permitted quite enough repose - until the train ride and the stroll through the city created a more relaxing rhythm to the day. He was acutely aware of a tired tenseness building up in his shoulders as he sat waiting. Again. Always waiting. He'd a case to solve, and well, there was Rachel. Not just a witness but a child he felt a considerable degree of responsibility and affection for.

He decided that instead of moaning to himself he should use the time in the waiting room to try to sift through the information that crowded into the blur of recollections that constituted his week. Sarge felt it significant in hindsight, that Nancy had taken her second anonymous call of the week. It bothered him. Most small-town folks who loved to phone-in bad news or reports of local goings-on were more than happy to identify themselves. Callers to Table Top police station were often excited by their scoop and were mostly up for a long chat about all and sundry, anyway. He and Nancy had scarcely taken two anonymous calls in a year, let alone two in one week. Could they be connected? The first anonymous call was to report an outsider watching the kids in the school yard. The second call was to report the accident.

Sarge rose up to stretch his cramping legs after the day's travel. He flowed into an adjoining courtyard through a teak and glass door. Inside was a most appealing space with greenery and even a small water feature. One might have expected that the officer would have been soothed by the sound of water filling and falling from the charming well at the centre of the room. Complete with lily-pads floating on the surface, the small pond was a picture of serenity. Instead, the policeman seemed to be growing increasingly agitated as he paced in the courtyard. He promptly removed himself back to the adjoining sitting room.

Sarge was feeling quite edgy by the tricking water - combined with the wait. Ever since he was a kid and had experienced flood waters, he'd been this way. His old man had taken him on a few family holidays to the farm where he himself had grown up and his father before him - in the vast north-west region. Several of the small holdings, and indeed townships, were built on flood plains. This proved no issue in times of drought yet when nature swung to the other extreme, as she was wont to do in Australia, Sarge confessed that he found the rising of flood waters unnerving, to say the least. Sarge understood that the rivers and creeks were naturally the life blood of such communities. He grasped that the bursting of waterways meant that feed became prolific to fatten stock and mineral deposits from flooding could be currency for numerous livelihoods dependent on cotton or wheat yields. High risk, but potentially high profits, was the way it worked out west. Farming wasn't the life he had wanted for himself. He'd known early on that living off the capriciousness of the land wasn't for him. Instead, he'd trained at Goulburn Police Academy. Any misgivings his family had about his career choice were stamped out as they proudly watched him march in his smart uniform at his graduation. Besides, it wasn't like his policing path had taken him to work undercover in some risky operation attempting to flush out a criminal gang. His career path had wound around gently to his post at Table Top.

Yet, in that impressionable space between boyhood and manhood, the reality of livelihoods, hopes and dreams all being linked to a floodplain, had made an indelible impression on him, when he experienced havoc from flash flooding after torrential rain unleashed itself. He'd seen waters come up in haste and recede just as quickly. Two years in a row he'd been conscripted to pull up rank, soggy carpet to be dried out in the steaming sun. Not much of a way to spend summer holidays, he thought. However, he did admit to himself at the time that he valued the easy camaraderie forged with his dad and granddad, as they worked shoulder-to-shoulder.

No, what was even worse was the flood of stealth, which he so despised. During another January of his adolescence, he'd experienced a different phenomenon - the slow and steady advance of flood waters, even after the storms and rains had ceased. 'The big wet' crept into the town in stages from upstream, over what had seemed the longest week of his life. Daily, areas which were dry in the morning were silently but surely underwater by the afternoon. Encroaching on the town stealthily, the waters encircled the town and at the same time insinuated itself through ovals and common spaces. They were safe but he didn't think it was much of a way to spend his school holidays. It was dull and hot, but what stressed him out immensely - probably testing the mettle of the entire community, was the slow silent creep of the water.

So too with this case, Sarge reflected. He felt unsettled in having to play a waiting game with his little witness, to extract evidence. He was far better suited to an emergency response, like when the mother and child were MIA. Give him hands-down any day, a flash flood that created a crisis which needed a response in real time. He much preferred that over the silent waiting game of a predicted, but gradual flooding. *Strike! Who needs a ruddy shrink, me or the kid?* he muttered, rousing himself from his introspection. *Probably those who wax lyrical about extreme weather conditions and then talk to themselves about it all,* came his prompt answer to himself - in true Aussie self-deprecation. The officer smirked at all this uncharacteristic mind traffic. So much so, that when the doctor opened the door separating her office from the waiting room, he was caught grinning like a manic Cheshire Cat.

"Private joke doc, don't you worry about me, though - it's debatable if I would make it in the comedy scene."

3

As her manner had promised over the phone, Doctor Christina King was warm and engaging. Sarge relaxed a little after only a few minutes. She had a knack for making people feel comfortable by defaulting to her own gentle and ironic humour.

"Not to be confused with the sister of the famous Doctor Martin Luther KING- yet I do deal in freedom fighting!" she had quipped with a grin, when introducing herself.

In appearance, she was unremarkable. She was neither attractive nor unattractive, young or old, tall or short, thin or overweight; neither pale nor ruddy. It seemed like Dr Chris adopted some neutral middle ground so as not to either dominate or distract her patients. Nonetheless, she projected an engaging but comfortable persona when interacting with people, which was far from bland. Like a seemingly nondescript car that would never attract attention to itself, it wasn't until one was in the passenger seat and experiencing how easily, yet masterfully, it cruised the open road, that the realisation came - you were in a remarkable, safe and capable vehicle.

Her voice was a little lower than most females and it had an almost musical intonation, which Sarge imagined would simultaneously captivate and soothe any of the children she counselled.

"May I please dispense with the formalities and call you Sarge?"

"Of course, doc, you're the boss," returned Sarge.

"Well, now that's established, I think we're going to get along just fine, Sarge," laughed Christina. "Don't mind me, facetious is my middle name," she winked. "In all seriousness, I don't see myself as a soloist, even though I bring my expertise to this situation. We work as a team, Sarge. You'll be a comforting presence, well, in the background at least, for the initial sessions I conduct with Rachel. I understand that you've already been handling things beautifully to make the child feel comfortable."

The sergeant smiled back at the doctor.

"Normally, I recommend casual dress and definitely no uniforms, which can intimidate children, except of course in this case - your uniform is associated with protection and normality. It's not every day that a child knows her local policeman, let alone as her rescuer. You, sir, are comfort and safety rolled into one package. Invaluable."

The blend of humour and sincerity Dr King managed to convey in her remarks worked like a balm for Sarge's tense stomach.

"Child psychologists agree - with appropriate questioning techniques, an eight -year-old can indeed recall and describe detailed memories of their recent experiences, even traumatic ones which will help you with your witness problem- and most importantly help Rachel deal with the barrage of unwelcome experiences that have been dumped on her in this last week.

Without boring you with too much 'psych-speak,' even kids who have a 'don't tell,' motto ingrained in their responses, can be helped. Even children who through trauma or manipulation, have adopted mutism, really want to be able to verbalise. Or at least they can be empowered to express their experience through other modes of communication than speech itself. Kids are truth-tellers, and their contribution, or in this case, their evidence, cannot be underestimated."

"Yep, you are preaching to the choir here doc. My own daughter can't help but say what she sees. She's happy to make her observations known to me. For instance, she is not backward in coming forwards in telling me that I have way too many donuts under my belt," Sarge chuckled.

Doctor King nodded ruefully. "Right. Kids naturally verbalise their perceptions and must learn guile and social niceties. Our job is to essentially continue to build rapport with Rachel and trust that one way or another,

Rachel will be able to assist you and provide clues to help you solve your case, which in turn will help me to help her process recent events."

"In your professional experience, how confident are you that she'll resume speech soon?"

Dr King hesitated. "Quite confident, if she can feel safe enough to break her silence. However, not knowing exactly all that Rachel has been through, I can only say that it's expected and not guaranteed. Hopefully, the inconvenience and frustration of not speaking in everyday, practical situations, will weigh on our side. Each day will bring Rachel fresh motivation to start speaking again. The trick is for us to get to the bottom of whatever manipulation or threats this little girl has been entangled in. Sarge, you made the right call to bring Rachel to Desmond House."

The child expert, also being highly proficient in reading men, paused to allow the police officer time to absorb her comments, knowing that most blokes benefitted from the assurance that they had made the right judgement call.

"Tell me doc, what should I expect? I mean, how will you run the sessions with Rach?"

"Great question. It's my opinion that just as childhood play is essential to development in the early years and precedes formal education, play will help Rachel learn to trust and speak in her current context. All our so-called 'therapy' here is child centred in this way. It's amazing what children will divulge when playing with cars or dolls. Yet the same child will clam up if they are interviewed in a grown-up way. Of course, drawings are sometimes very informative when kids are going through a non-verbal patch, as well. Tell me Sarge, are you much of a talker at home with your wife? Don't worry, I'm not psychoanalysing you and there is no wrong or right answer, I promise."

"Well," Sarge drawled, "around the dinner table we all chat as Anna witters on like a magpie, but if I'm honest, if my wife asks me directly about how I feel about something, I kinda clam up. Not trying to be difficult, but I just can't think of what to say in those moments."

"Right, you and many husbands. When do you think you tend to chat or share a bit more freely? And I recognise that using the word *share* here could automatically make you cringe or feel pressured," Christina said with a twinkle in her eye as she adjusted her spectacles more comfortably on her nose.

Sarge stared at the psychologist for a moment.

"Got me there," he admitted, "guilty as charged. I reckon I just go blank or even feel a bit panicked if wifey puts the squeeze on me to *share* something about my feelings with her, direct-like. Even being asked to make a spot decision can make me break a sweat," he grinned. "Especially when I don't know the right answer to give that'll keep the peace."

The psychologist waited.

"I guess when we're gardening together, I sometimes talk a bit about things. Or when we go on holidays and I do a long drive with Anna asleep in the back and Sarah at my side, and nothing but the road stretching ahead... yeah, then we have big chats."

"You and a lot of husbands operate like that."

"Is that right?"

"Very common. Well, we call that *horizontal communication* in my field. Many relationship dynamics contribute to communication occurring best when people are alongside one another. As you have just described, you know, when a couple are enjoying something relaxing and recreational together, just being companionable can loosen the tongue for those who'd run a mile rather than sit down face-to-face and bare their souls. Well, 'play therapy' is just another example of horizontal communication."

"Makes sense to me."

Sarge felt some of the shoulder tension and stomach upset that had gripped him, slowly dissipate. This lady knew what she was doing.

"Is there anything I should know about what I do or don't do in these play-therapy sessions? I don't wanna detract from what you are doing by acting awkward or getting in the way."

Christina smiled at Sarge. "We don't script that too much. Just take a seat somewhere in the Red Room - which is where we'll meet after dinner tonight. The children eat early, so let's meet there at 6:30 pm. It's not an office but an enormous play room. When you come with Rachel, just do whatever feels natural. Sit where you like. Play with Rachel if she initiates it or includes you."

"Go in with the mindset that you're permitted to be present in sessions, both as Rachel's security blanket and discreetly, as the investigating officer. No need to have your notebook out, as the sessions will be recorded. Recording is not possible, however, so it is important that you're in the sessions to observe Rachel's non-verbal communication as I interact with her and build up to *conversation* of some sort."

"Here's hoping."

"As you'll see, we don't work with the children in conventional office spaces. You won't find me behind a desk. In fact, you might enjoy playing in the Red Room too. Relax, but be alert," she reassured the officer. "As I said, interact with Rachel in the play space if she invites it, otherwise just find a spot that you feel is adequate to your role as observer, and be as normal as you can be," she grinned.

"Normal, yup. Being normal and boring, is my regular gig."

"No need to play good cop or bad cop," she winked. "Just follow my cues."

Sarge chuckled. "Doc, we don't tend to play games in our district interviews. Even with repeat offenders who are adults, and scum at that ... bullying or agro questioning are methods reserved for prime-time crime shows. No point getting hot and bothered with theatrics. I'm a straight up and down copper. Would probably outsmart myself in any mind games I tried to pull. With witnesses, especially those who are children, even the most disillusioned officer I know is only gonna go softly, softly."

Sarge stopped. Clearly, he thought, this lady had loosened his tongue. He never ran on like this. Rachel was gonna be in good hands with Dr King and he sincerely hoped she'd be prattling on like her previous self in no time.

"Just be assured, Sarge, your presence plays a crucial role in making this child feel comfortable in this new space and mixing with strangers. It helps me build rapport with her more quickly. You're the bridge between us. We've lots of tools in our toolbox as therapists, but essentially, we can't make any progress until the patient feels safe and at ease. Once we achieve that, I have every confidence that with appropriate questioning techniques, this eight-year-old can indeed recall and describe important details of her recent experience, one way or another."

"That would be most helpful."

"Yes. I can appreciate what is at stake here. I have extended my working day for this very purpose. After an early dinner I will see Rachel for her first session. Dinner is served at 6pm in the meals room. There's a map in your rooms which will assist you when navigating your way through the labyrinth of Desmond House. Here's one you can take with you." The doctor handed him a map to take with him, at which he frowned and squinted simultaneously.

"You'll find your way as easily as an annoying relative who outstays Christmas lunch," Christina joked.

"An all too familiar picture in my clan," said Sarge.

Christina grinned and nodded knowingly.

4

Sarge took the opportunity after the meeting to get out for a stroll and enjoy the cool sea breeze as dusk approached, with Rachel as his willing companion. This both allowed Liza to freshen up with only herself to be concerned with and offered a public space for him to be with the child. They only had to cross the road to walk along the beach, which was breathtaking in the soft pink light. He'd enjoyed the time with the psychologist, and it had given the earnest policeman a good deal to think about. He always found this part of day- the gloaming -a time where he defaulted to pensive reflection. The shifting in time between afternoon and evening shifted obstacles in his brain. On this occasion he was both thoughtful and thankful. Marvelling at the turn of events which had taken him from country to coast, he could imagine that it was an enormous thing for an eight-year-old to take on board. He worried that the separation from her town and friends was cruel, on top of everything else Rachel was contending with.

He watched Rachel drink deeply from a water fountain and then skip and weave her way along the boardwalk. He was relieved to see her abandoned in her response to this stimulating new environment. Her enjoyment was contagious. He loved that about kids, and his own daughter in particular, who translated him into so many social settings. Kids could convert the mundane into the magical with their eager smiles and innocent play. It dawned on him that Rachel had added a new lens through which he now saw the world. Her story was leaving an indelible mark on him.

He quickened his pace to keep up with the nimble little girl who had momentarily disappeared. Rounding the slight curve in the path, he saw that Rachel had merely ducked under the overhang of a rock as she panted and paused to catch her breath. With his heart in his throat, he felt a surge of protectiveness which he knew was deeper than professionalism, as he recalled that charmed moment when Rachel emerged from her rocky hiding place just last Tuesday at a similar time of day to this.

Rescuing Rachel would always be a true highlight of his life. Yet there was something else lapping at his thoughts, like the relentless waves he could hear as the tide came in only metres away from the path. Beyond the *feel-good* vibes of finding a lost child there was an added sense of wonder. He stood appreciating the marvel of sky and sea stretching out before him. Was it the wonder of creation? He tried to rationalise this feeling that pressed upon him. Suddenly he understood. He was experiencing a strong sensation - pressing on him was the growing realisation that he'd indeed been used by a power bigger than himself, to bring a child to safety. This insight had been hovering at the edges of his mind all week.

Transported back to his wayward antics in Sunday school, he remembered the kindly lady who after the hymns were sung, took on all the boisterous boys who'd been quivering with pent up energy in the pews. This sainted lady was both fun and patient. She was able to look past all their naughtiness and loudness, telling them wonderful stories of God's love. And she showed it. He realised with surprise that he'd retained much of her teaching. She'd framed the Easter story as God's great rescue plan for all, which appealed to his sense of adventure. In hindsight, he wondered if the strange sense he'd experienced throughout the long afternoon searching at Budginigi, was an experience of receiving help from above. Had his involvement in the rescues last week caused him to sub-consciously ponder the Rescuer?

*A very present help in a time of trouble.* A long-ago text drifted back to him.

He sheepishly feared that he was going soft, imagining spiritual experiences. What a notion! Still, he wondered if it was time to get back to church. It occurred to him that he would like Anna to experience what he had in his childhood but grew away from. Perhaps this train of thought had also been encouraged by some of what he saw in the waiting room. The brochure had indicated that this whole place was instigated by a clergyman who had recuperated at Manly Beach. He hadn't been so long away from his faith to recognise that the cross-stitched words in the sampler on the wall were a reference from somewhere in the Gospels. He still had a visual stuck in his head from the *Uncle Arthur Bedtime Stories* he was read as a kid. Kindly, all-encompassing Jesus, resplendent in a joyful light, gathered the small children around him. Sarge supposed he was long overdue to get back to his roots. He felt remiss in not giving Anna access to a church community. There was a small chapel service held every second week at Table Top. If his shift work didn't get in the way, and if the wife didn't object, he would endeavour to attend the service with his little family. At very least, he ruminated, he might dig out those old bedtime stories from the boxed-up remnants of his childhood in the garage and read them to Anna.

The policeman mused that if nothing else, this extraordinary situation with little Rachel at the centre of it had brought a swell of introspection and opportunity into his previously stagnant life.

# Child and Psychologist

They meandered to the Red Room after a dinner where Sarge dined well, but Rachel ate sparingly. Dr King was already there, seated on a splendid round rug and absorbed with building a house on a low Lego table. Aptly named the 'Red Room' because of its plush yet playful *rouge* trimmings. Nothing was placed along the back of this enormously proportioned space. Instead, the rear wall housed floor to ceiling wallpaper featuring two wooden Beef Eaters, book-ending a charming Medieval toy castle scene. Their merry faces were not completely obscured by their fluffy helmets. No rifle was to be found in the hand of either toy soldier, but instead they juggled a delicious array of jellies and iced cupcakes. Happy flags flew from ramparts in this charming scene. Climbing red and white roses burst into paths of colour around corners of stone.

What child was not going to delve into this delightful den?

Christina sat shaking a fistful of brightly coloured bricks, improvising percussion to accompany the song she was singing.

Sarge recognised snatches of a chorus from a long gone *Top 40* hit.

*It's my party, I'll cry if I want to...* (shake, shake).

The doctor would look critically at her construction, head cocked to one side, and place a few more Lego pieces.

*(shake, shake) You would cry too, if it happened to you.*

*Hmm... hmmm... hmmm...* (shake, shake) *hmmm... hmmm... if it happened to you.*

Rachel surveyed the scene before her for a minute more, then ran over and sat on the rug.

The psychologist crooned more softly and then ceased her song, smiling at Rachel who rummaged amongst the mountain of Lego bricks, carefully selecting a few. Rachel moved towards Christina's creation, stopping short of adding a window to an unfinished wall.

The child looked expectantly at the lady next to her.

"Go right ahead. What lovely manners you have."

Rachel now smiled at Christina shyly. They sat harmoniously building in silence for a good ten minutes. Rachel abruptly looked up at her new playmate, suddenly unable to hide her curiosity.

"I'm Miss Chris, Rachel. Welcome to Desmond House. I am a child doctor who loves to help children like you feel confident and safe to communicate again. This is my favourite room in the whole place!"

She stopped to look around the room and beam. Rachel followed her eyes, smiling appreciatively at what the doctor was looking at.

"Thanks for stopping by before bedtime to have a play…you aren't too tired after your long trip on the train, are you?" she enquired with mock anxiety, a twinkle in her eye.

The child shook her head emphatically.

"Ah…good. Glad you want to stay up a little longer."

They sat companionably. The only sound was the trowelling of hands sifting through Lego bricks. Eventually, the psychologist resumed humming the hit song. On one or two occasions Rachel hummed along too, not even aware that she was doing it.

Sarge had seated himself on a bean bag nestled in between the low L-shaped bookshelves at the side of the room. He raised an eyebrow, all that he would allow himself to betray his excitement at this minor breakthrough. For all the days which had elapsed since the accident, this was the only sound he had heard pass Rachel's lips, other than the giggles she had shared with Anna.

 "It must be getting close to bedtime. Maybe we have time for one more thing. Would you like to play some more with me?"

Rachel shrugged her shoulders with reservation.

"Smart cookie," said Dr King. "Of course, you want to know what we are going to do before you agree to anything! Do you like puzzles?"

Rachel vigorously nodded her assent.

Dr King bounced up and crossed to a cupboard just inside the door they had come in. The child had not yet even noted its existence. There was so much for her eyes, wide with interest, to take in. Returning to the round mat with a box and other things tucked under her arm, Miss Chris sat down with a flounce, tucking her floral, flowing skirt around her ankles in one motion.

"I have a kitten at home which looks a bit like this cute little guy," she said, showing the child the lid of the puzzle box which featured an adorable white kitten with iridescent blue eyes set against a backdrop off tangled coloured yarns. "Shall we take turns with the pieces?"

Rachel nodded and indicated to her playmate that she should go first.

"Thank you, I will."

The small girl nodded in agreement. They sat peacefully as they concentrated on the puzzle before them. At times, both lapsed into humming snatches of the song Miss Chris had been crooning at the beginning of the play session.

Dr King did not react in any way at all, let alone indicate that a minor miracle has taken place. Professionalism and patience were her hallmarks.

It's possible that Rachel hadn't even comprehended that she was verbalising (in a manner of speaking), so intent was she on solving the jigsaw in front of them. Or, maybe she did realise, but was feeling relaxed and comfortable enough to allow the lapse.

Rachel was fighting a valiant battle to concentrate, due to the weariness which was overtaking her. She failed in stifling a yawn, as much as she tried.

Sarge shifted in his seat in the bean bag, Rachel arranged the final puzzle piece just-so and compared the vivid picture they had formed together, with the one on the jigsaw puzzle box.

"Genius!" Miss Chris announces with glee.

Rachel smiled with satisfaction.

"Well, I can see that you're good at doing jigsaws, Rachel. If you think of it, Sarge has an important sort of puzzle he must solve too. Would you be able to help him put his puzzle pieces together? Would you like to do that Rachel?"

Rachel looked at Christina King quizzically. It was as if she has been tasked with working the expert out.

"Here is an art book and some markers for you to keep. It's time to go back to your room now, but why don't we ask Liza if it's okay that you have a little bit of time to draw before lights out?"

Even from a distance, Sarge could detect a definite gleam in the child's eyes. Sleepy Rachel still embraced just a little more play time before lights out.

"After you get ready for bed maybe you could open this new art book and write your name in fancy letters? It'll be there for you on your desk whenever you want to doodle or draw. When you are ready, you could draw a picture or write some words that you think will help Sarge find the driver of the car that hit you and Mummy. If that person told you that you couldn't tell … I bet he didn't say that you couldn't write or draw?" Miss Chris stated this last part with reassuring confidence.

Rachel considered this insight thoughtfully.

Miss Chris went on softly. "Thank goodness you and mum are both safe now. The doctors are going to wake mummy up as soon as her head is better.

It's just that Sarge needs to solve his puzzle so he can finish off all his boring paperwork."

Rachel didn't make eye-contact with either of them, but she opened her arms happily to receive the pad with thick paper and the felt-tip markers. She looked appreciatively at the gift. She wasn't always allowed to draw or write with anything other than pencils or crayons. At school she didn't have her pen license yet.

Miss Chris reiterated, "I know you don't want to speak about what happened, Rachel and you know what? You don't have to speak if you don't want to, but I'd like you to know that it's safe for you to create a picture."

Miss Chris observed a mixture of caginess and relief in Rachel's eyes.

# Rachel

1

In the dining room the next morning Rachel sat silently at the round table, seemingly still, but underneath the table cloth she was clutching and then scrunching her pinafore to the beat of a loved choir melody in her head. She couldn't banish the lyric - *Consider yourself at home, consider yourself part of the furniture*, from playing again and again in her head. Her eyes darted to and fro as she watched all the bustle in the bright and airy breakfast room. At first, she was soothed by the clatter of cutlery, the lines filing past the servery and people at tables, who didn't seem concerned with her at all. It reminded her of those moments at the end of recess, before the bell sounded, when everyone scuffled around, stowing away their wrappers in their backpacks, taking one last swig from their drink bottles and tossing orange peel to the waiting magpies.

She was happy to be inconspicuous for a while, in amongst the routine of the dining room which has diverted the concentration of her minders. All the unusual attention she had been receiving had made her feel on edge today. She had woken up feeling vaguely worried. The child psychologist might identify Rachel's state as feeling vulnerable and exposed, but Rachel would simply conclude that she was feeling homesick.

*Consider yourself at home, consider yourself part of the furniture.*

She wasn't at home, even if the snatches of the song stuck in her brain, told her so repeatedly. To make matters even worse, Rachel's reverie was rudely interrupted by an audible savage growl coming from her empty stomach. The child frowned. Food was a problem. She'd suffered the bland dinner she'd only picked at the night before. She was less than pleased with the breakfast options before her. She normally never ate soggy *Rice Bubbles*. She cast a disdainful eye at the hot food on offer. Rachel pushed the anaemic and congealing scrambled egg around her plate.

*How can toast be toast if its limp and cold?*

It was a mystery to Rachel how these grown-ups with their hairnets and aprons, moving around the kitchen so professionally, could mess up something so simple. The tepid, spongey bread stuck in her throat. Rachel gagged. Not even the spreads on offer tempted her.

At home, when they'd run out of money, and the next pension day hadn't yet arrived, Mum would declare, "We'll never starve as long as I can fry you an egg or make us some pancakes!"

Their eggs at home were bright yellow, some produced double yokes. Even the bantam chicks who laid tiny eggs still offered up flavoursome morsels.

She watched the policeman. Sarge seemed oblivious to the fact that he was gustily consuming a substandard meal. Rachel stared at him as he wiped up the bacon grease and sauce on his plate with his last crust, washing it all down with his third cup of scalding black tea. Scraping his chair back, he headed over to the servery for a quick survey of any further helpings. Liza left to go back to the room to freshen up.

Rachel shrunk down into her chair- her head not that much higher than the table with its sticky plastic tablecloth. She looked carefully from side to side. In one swift movement, she noiselessly slid off the chair and disappeared.

The child was light on her feet and used to making herself scarce when required. In her view, this occasion required it. She seamlessly exited via the back door, finding herself in a service courtyard with waste bins in one corner and a mop and bucket in another. There was a passage leading to who knows where, on the far side. Rachel heard voices and the squeak of the door adjacent to the one she had just come out of. She was already on top of the rectangular dumpster before the door slammed shut. Deftly, she climbed onto the low sloping roof of what might be a storeroom. She loved climbing. Once, before they had moved to Table Top, she had given her mother quite a scare. Rachel had been reluctant to have her requisite rest in her bedroom. There had been a volley of raised voices. When Mum had flopped herself back on the couch in front of a daytime soap opera, Rachel had silently slipped out the front door and run away. She didn't go that far, but Tess didn't know that. With great fascination, Rachel watched from the arms of a trusty oak tree, the people scurrying and searching up and down the street. She heard neighbours calling her name. It was several hours before she decided it was best to creep back down and present herself.

Rachel lay flat on the roof listening to occasional remarks about the weather from two kitchen workers on a smoke break. It amused her that she could see them, yet they were unaware of her presence. She felt both invisible and invincible in that instant. It was the first time she'd been by herself since last week, when she was home from school with the mumps, resting in her room alone ... or of course, when she was hiding in the bush. Oh, it seemed such a long time ago now!

What a relief! It felt good not being supervised or scrutinised for a change. She watched the clouds slowly scuttle across the blue sky contentedly.

After a while though, the unpleasant smell emanating from a nearby drain -like sour milk- and the fetid stink of garbage fermenting in Sydney's humidity, drove her down. This hideaway did not compare to the fresh breeze whistling through her grass tunnels on Burma Road.

She followed the alleyway around old red-brick walls, out to a lovely courtyard. She arranged herself on a wrought iron and wood bench seat and watched the water feature in the centre.

A receptionist spied her, sitting cross-legged on the bench, chin in her hands, mesmerised by the twisting water that had no beginning or end. Shortly after, Miss Chris came out of another door opening into the courtyard. She had a bright beach ball under her arm. She paid no mind to Rachel but seems intent on crossing the courtyard, preoccupied with her own thoughts. As she passed the still child, she nonchalantly dropped the beach ball. Rachel instinctively fetched it and threw it back to Miss Chris. She returned it to Rachel and for at least a minute they passed the ball backwards and forwards. In mock defeat, Miss Chris retrieved the ball which had rolled under the bench. She held her hand out to Rachel who smiled and placed her hand in hers. She obediently went with this lady who was so very nice.

Sarge and Liza looked very relieved to see Rachel but didn't fuss or ask her where she had been. Rachel sat at the desk in her room drawing a new picture in her art book while the grown-ups chatted in the corridor.

2

It was decided after this quick consult, that Rachel should go on an outing where nothing was expected of her, and that her next session with Dr King be rescheduled until later in the afternoon. Dr King suggested a beach walk and lunch out with Sarge and Liza, as a circuit breaker for the wave of homesickness that had likely washed over the little girl.

The ordinarily unlikely companions ventured out on a very sticky Sydney day. The hope of a sea breeze propelled them to the water. Chatting to Rachel, Liza was anxious to distract her before the child retreated into her previous pale misery, by the offer of exploring along the rocks and perhaps an ice-cream at the place they had walked past just a day ago. Liza chattered about how well she knew and loved Manly. She told Rachel that when she was just eighteen years old, she moved from a small town to study and live in a musty, cramped terrace in Surry Hills, with two other students. Rachel could tell that Liza loved her university days. She talked of how she and her friends would take the ferry over on fine weekends. Liza explained that she still found time to go on wonderful outings, even when she was madly working to make rent and studying for her degree.

Rachel was keenly interested in this concept of going to school as a grown up. Mummy didn't get to finish school, and Rachel thought that this made her sad. She could well understand this, as she herself adored school. However, the previously unfamiliar notion of higher education captivated Rachel momentarily and broadened her horizons in a way that nothing else had up until this point in her life. She wondered if she would get to go to college.

The beauty of the day soon distracted Rachel from thoughts of her further education, pulling her back to the present. She inhaled the air which was thick and sultry. A faint breeze ruffled her hair. She was such a tumble of introspection and sensory seeking.

After wordlessly admiring the dazzle of sunlight intersecting with the turquoise waters off Manly Beach, without articulating their intentions, Sarge, Rachel and Liza drifted to the beach to wet their toes. Rachel and Sarge naturally distanced themselves from the crowds of families congregating around the safety of the flags. They were used to open spaces.

Rachel stopped for some time at a stack of surfboards before they rounded the point. Mouth open she stared, mesmerised by the figures riding the waves. She didn't like being jostled by the crush of sun-seekers weaving around her, so she reluctantly cut short her scrutiny of the surfers' skill.

Moving past the giant cement steps, they rounded the curve slowly. Rachel gaped at the towering red brick apartments to her right, and the stunning coastline to her left. Whipping her head from side to side, she picked up speed and wove her way between the white railing separating her from the sea on one side and the natural sandstone hidey-holes sculpted by tide and time, on the other. Sarge and Liza gave Rachel full reign as they meandered along behind her. Smiling, they watched as Rachel cantered and careered along the pathway ahead. Liza playfully made a mock show of chasing her until Rachel conceded defeat and stayed at the water fountain, gulping for ages. It was humid even in the breeze and the social worker flopped herself down on a seat facing the panoramic beach framed by the wooden railings she was gazing through.

Sarge leant on the same long line of railings once he had reached the top of the incline. In between panting, he reflected on how the kid had gotten under his skin. She'd infiltrated some of the barriers he'd carefully erected over a lifetime.

Liza stood up, after admiring the view for ten minutes from a seated position. She broke into the policeman's reverie.

"Letting Rachel take control of how she spends this time could be therapy in itself with all the change that has been thrust upon her."

Sarge was in total agreement but said little as he sweated in the sun. Rachel waiting and watching ahead.

Her mind telegraphed: *Hurry up slow pokes!*

Liza and Sarge received Rachel's message. Laughing, they tried to catch up to her. The littlest member of the party led the way. She found a perfect spot to duck through the coast fence to a rock platform almost level with the path. Gesturing for the adults to follow, she expertly found pathways along rock or sand or when required, she nimbly leapt from rock to rock. A most wonderful hour was spent gently poking barnacles and starfish as they clambered over boulders. The tide was out so Rachel's playground was a relatively safe one. They splashed in shallow pools left by the retreating sea as a fresh breeze blew away the cloying, close air which had blanketed them for much of the time since they emerged from Desmond House. Rachel quickly became overconfident with the terrain, which was both new and exciting, but also reminiscent of her beloved hills at home. She disappeared for a few minutes, which prompted her minders to increase their efforts to keep pace with their charge. She miscalculated the distance between two rocks when bounding over a gap and scraped her knees and hands as she scrambled to retrieve her place on the rocks. A shadow flitted across the eight- year- old's carefree countenance.

They wandered on to Shelly Beach and Rachel looked carefully at all the signs - quite an old soul with a child's face. They read about the species of marine life and flora which proliferated in and were protected in the entire Cabbage Tree Bay precinct. Rachel paused at a sign detailing the Manly scenic walkways, hastily Liza stepped in and explained that this was a big afternoon excursion, and not an option for today. Rachel accepted this without fuss and nodded in agreement when the social worker intimated that lunch might be a priority. Naturally, it was hard to resist making souvenirs from a couple of particularly pretty shells before they doubled back, finding it much quicker progress when travelling via the path instead of along the rocks.

However, moving anywhere with a child seemed slow going by Sarge's reckoning. Nonetheless, he looked on indulgently as Rachel stopped to inspect each and every plaque which dotted the walkway-which listed the native vegetation that lined the reserve, labelled with their correct botanical names. Rachel took extra time at the *Livistona australis* plaque, the Latin term for "Cabbage Tree Palm," the namesake of the beautiful bay they'd been looking at ahead.

The policeman's patience was rewarded when he realised that Rachel was mouthing the words, trying to read and pronounce them and he caught her whispering the phrase. She turned and made eye contact with Sarge, and he nodded in a matter-of-fact way, reassuring the child.

"Sounds right to me kiddo…or should I say, your Latin name- *Girlius australis?*"

Rachel disintegrated into peals of laughter which were contagious.

Liza, quick as a whip, joined in, without any fanfare to signify what was a perceptible moment in the child's recovery process.

"Ha! *Filius* might be more accurate… or that might be for a boy, not a girl? It's sadly been a long time since my high school Latin classes, in which I could have concentrated a bit better."

After that, every so often one of the adults would point and give ridiculous faux- Latin names to mundane objects and set them all off giggling again.

Sarge looked at his watch and made a mental note, which he would later transcribe to his police notebook:

*11:52: Child witness articulates quietly for the first time since the hit-and-run.*

He looked forward to passing news of this development onto the child psychologist.

The trio headed north, passing Desmond House, drawn to the lively music spilling from the mall. Rachel appeared to tense until they passed the children's home, clearly not ready to enter its confines yet, and wanting to be out wandering as they were, soaking up the stunning day.

The Corso, bookended by water in opposite directions, provided ample pleasant places to explore for any visitor checked into Desmond House. Manly Wharf with views out to Sydney Harbour was at one end of the mall, and the spectacular sweep of Manly Beach at the other. The tidal pool down from the Ferry Station, enclosed with shark nets and bordered by an inviting curve of sand, was a magnet for the country people adjusting to beach conditions. The absence of waves other than the intermittent movement created by the ferries, made the pool more relaxing and safer for inexperienced swimmers. The beach with its red and yellow surf lifesaving flags, was only across the road from Desmond House and could be accessed safely by the pedestrian crossing which bridged the busy road separating them. However, the children from the facility were always taken to the tidal pool to swim, instead of the open sea. The home had a sun-blessed, extensive playground at its steps.

Happy to be moving out of the sun, the trio wove along the Corso seeking shade from the shop awnings and the riot of cabbage palms and pines crowding the centre of the walkway. Sarge and the social worker readily took up Rachel's suggestion when she tugged on Sarge's hand and pointed at a blue sign with a faded but unmistakable picture of a fish. The smell of frying food was tantalising. Rachel's appetite was revived by the fresh salt air and delicious aroma.

They rambled along nearby, waiting with anticipation for lunch to be prepared. Rachel bobbed into the public phone box in the centre of the mall. The door protested, squeaking as she opened it. Pushing the metal flap of the coin refund, she carefully searched for forgotten coins. Finding none, she examined every inch of the compartment until she was rewarded by spotting the dull copper of an abandoned two cent piece in the corner of the cement slab. Triumphant, she pocketed her find and adeptly manoeuvred the door, removing herself from what was really a steaming hot box with the sun directly hitting the glass and metal. Sweating, but smiling, she rejoined the adults.

Liza caught Sarge's eye which, like her, showed amusement at the scenario which had just unfolded. Unbeknownst to them, in the avid pursuit of pocket money, Rachel Moloney had previously adapted all sorts of resourceful ways of scrounging for change before they'd moved to Table Top - some honest and some not. Living in a village location afforded no phone boxes on street corners, nor were there corner stores at Table Top, so Rachel was loving the possibilities of the city.

Rachel sat in the shade remembering shared rituals with the other neighbourhood kids. In the housing commission suburb she'd lived in, prior to coming to Table Top, in the searing summer evenings after tea, tiny children were permitted to roam in packs and walk barefoot in the shimmering heat the few hundred meters to the corner shop - clutching coins for confectionery. Rachel would queue and jostle, awaiting her turn to choose mixed lollies. Afterward they would do handstands and play Tag on whichever front lawn was greenest and had the least bindi-eyes to prick their feet. Rachel knew the code like all the kids did, as soon as the first streetlight came on, it was time to return home. Bath time saw her soaking in cold water, as air-conditioning was not a feature in most houses in the seventies. It wasn't uncommon for her and her playmates to spend ages scrubbing tar off their feet in those halcyon summer evenings, when the bitumen road had grown so hot to turn to liquid and stick to already grubby, calloused feet.

"Number 22," bellowed the shop assistant.

All three of them jumped to attention as their lunch order was called. Rachel followed the policeman as he stepped up to the counter to pay and claim their wonderful smelling parcel wrapped in butcher's paper. She solemnly offered him her recently claimed treasure.

"Lunch is on me kiddo. Your shout next time," he winked.

Doubling back across Steyne Street they claimed a spot in the shade with a modicum of sea breeze. They chose a beach hut in which to lunch, which commanded a fine view of the stretch of Manly Beach. In no time at all they devoured their fish and chips, with chunks of lemon to squeeze over the delicious food. Ever vigilant to defend their meal from a growing number of hopeful seagulls, they ate quickly, undeterred by their audience.

Skipping back to Desmond House, Rachel sensed Liza and Sarge smiling at each other over her head, she felt pleased that they had relished the fish and chips they'd shared together. Finally, some decent food!

3

Relaxed and no longer hungry, Rachel veritably bounded into her appointment with Miss Chris. Clutching her art book, she halted in front of the doctor and solemnly handed it over to her with all the dignity of a velvet-clad page offering a scroll to a monarch. This time they were meeting in the courtyard because the playrooms were all occupied.

"Thank you for the drawing, Rachel. Is this a special picture of something that you remember from the accident?"

Rachel nodded earnestly.

"Shall we look at it together?"

By way of an answer, Rachel climbed onto the smooth wooden seat next to Christina and scooted over, almost touching her.

Miss Chris lifted the cover on the sketch pad. Inside was a colourful drawing of a bee and a butterfly. Even though the child had clearly enjoyed using the bright markers, the gaiety of the picture was undermined by the bold black lines Rachel had drawn all around the features and emanating from the insects, to form her background. Christina resettled her glasses which had slipped down her nose and peered carefully at the bee and butterfly. There were no smiles on these bright beauties, but instead grimaces, made with straight lines.

Looking encouragingly at Rachel, Miss Chris observed conversationally that the creatures did not look particularly friendly.

"What sort of faces are these?" she asked Rachel.

Rachel pulled her best cranky, angry expression.

The therapist nodded.

"Yes, you're quite good at drawing Rachel, I can see that this is a mean bee and butterfly,

even though they are still beautiful to look at. Are you able to tell me the story of this bee and butterfly and what they were doing at the accident? Sarge would love any help as he looks for clues. It's important to find the person who caused the accident when Mum was hurt."

Rachel looked earnest. She sucked in her breath just like any child does when they're about to launch into an eager explanation, but then suddenly stopped, shook her head whilst rasping, "not a word."

She looked shocked and then frightened by her own admission. Her eyes pooled with tears, her head jerking from side-to-side.

Miss Chris drew her arm around the child, who didn't resist, but nestled into Christina instead. They sat like that for a few minutes just watching the water tumble and fall. Eventually, Miss Chris handed Rachel a tissue to mop up the tears that had silently fallen.

She pulled out an orange bucket that had been under the bench all along and invited Rachel to help look after the Coi that were swimming in the pond. Together they fed the fish. Then, with small nets they scooped out floating leaves scattered from the nearby potted ornamental figs.

As they pottered around the pond together, Miss Chris gently chatted to Rachel, telling her she was in a safe place, that she was brave, that she was proud of her and that when she was ready, she could speak up or use other ways to 'speak' if she was more comfortable with them. They settled back onto the bench. Dr Chris produced some juice and cookies which had been obscured by her ample skirt. They sat munching comfortably.

"Rachel," Christina asked thoughtfully, "did the driver of the other car in the accident tell you that you couldn't tell anyone anything about him?"

Rachel agreed tacitly.

"The police think it was a male, is that right?"

The child nodded.

"Do you know him?"

She shook her head uncertainly.

Turning to face Rachel fully and smiling kindly, Miss Chris asked in a neutral tone, "Did he tell you that if you told anyone anything you saw, that something bad would happen?"

At this, Rachel looked incredulous that this lady before her could possibly know this secret information that had bound her so tightly. She nodded gravely. Her expression switched to guilty and cagey.

Miss Chris sensed that the child has reached a point that they would not progress beyond. Rachel would need to process what she had just given away and its repercussions.

Rachel suddenly looked exhausted, her shoulders sagging. When asked if she'd like to go and lie down, she looked immensely relieved. Sliding down the seat, she placed her hand in Sarge's when he appeared from where he had been unobtrusively listening, in a green alcove across the courtyard. They trotted off to her room where Sarge laid a blanket over the child as she settled atop of her bed. Gruffly, but with affection, he told her what a top kid she was. She smiled and slept. He stood protectively by the door for some time, whilst he updated his police notebook carefully.

4

Rachel couldn't be fully roused for dinner the next hour and could only be coaxed to drink half a glass of milk before she melted back into her slumber. She slept and slept through the night with Liza checking her regularly. At one stage, Liza worried that Rachel was running a bit hot, and she called the night nurse, fearing that the child may have lapsed back into high temperatures indicative of mumps or some other nasty childhood disease. The nurse bustled in, not at all perturbed at the hour and popped a thermometer under Rachel's arm. Ever so gently she felt the child's glands for any swelling. After updating Rachel's chart, the nurse reassured the social worker that Rachel was well enough, and that no doubt she was sleeping off the cumulative shock of all that her mind and emotions were grappling with.

The next morning it was agreed that Sarge could be spared now that Rachel had adjusted to her environment and bonded with Miss Chris. It was time for the police officer to return to the scene of the crime, as it were. Triplicate copies were taken of Rachel's artwork, to contribute to the files held at Desmond House, Community Services and the New South Wales Police. The police officer naturally took the original drawing with him in a protective plastic sleeve as the first evidence provided by his small witness. Carefully arranging Rachel Moloney's case notes provided from her sessions with the psychologist in his briefcase, Sarge locked it decisively and made his way downstairs to join Liza and Rachel in the breakfast room.

Fresh and smiling, this time Rachel was content to work her way through the selection of fresh fruit provided in the bowl next to the buffet of soggy cooked selections she had spurned the day previous and still ignored. Rachel listened happily enough to the chatter around her as she crunched on an apple with Liza at her side. She seemed to accept that Sarge must get back to the station to continue his investigations. He also explained that he needed to look after the Table Top community as he was the only officer of the law, and that he very much needed to see his family. At this Rachel nodded and smiled in understanding, knowing that Anna would be looking forward to her dad coming home. Liza would stay on with her for another day or so.

Child Services in consultation with Liza's feedback and the report from Dr King, had together decided that Rachel was best cared for by remaining at Desmond House for the time being. Either way, until Rachel's mother had recovered and was well enough to care for her young daughter, or until Rachel resumed the habit of talking again, there was no point in Rachel going back yet. Home would not represent normalcy and was closer to Rachel's fears and worries. The child would surely benefit from ongoing therapy and support.

Rachel would transition to the dormitory and receive lessons for a couple of hours each morning, along with other children booked into the long-stay program, so she didn't fall behind. Subtraction was the main area she needed drills in, her schoolteacher Mr Holden had reported. Her literacy skills were highly advanced for a child of her age. Fortunately, Rachel was up to date with her schoolwork and in almost all areas, was doing work for older grades. The child seemed excited to be told that she would do some lessons and that almost all afternoons, there would be free time. She could choose between glorious activities like swimming, exploring the rocks, and walking along Manly Beach. Not to mention handball, table tennis and time in the playrooms when the weather was not fine.

Sarge called past the upstairs short-stay room where Rachel was sitting at the desk, absorbed with her markers and pad, the remnant of Junior Scrabble nearby. *T E E N A G E R,* was spread across double and triple letter squares. Rachel shyly handed Sarge a picture with Anna's name neatly printed at the bottom. She'd drawn a ring of giant pine trees with a few girls playing underneath. One was skipping while others held the wide arc of rope at each end. The girl in the middle wore a bright red ribbon in her ponytail. Not hard to identify, as his daughter always wore a ribbon in her brown hair. Rachel Moloney by contrast, wore her white, blonde hair in a short, fashionable pageboy cut.

"Ah," he said delightedly, "that's my Anna skipping and that's you helping to turn the rope?"

Rachel nodded her assent cheerfully and Sarge promised to give it to Anna that night. The policeman said goodbye and embraced Rachel. She hugged him back tightly. He stopped at the doorway and gave her a final wave.

Sarge was very keen to get back and see his own daughter. Anna had come to them later in life than expected - like a wonderful rainbow after the rain. They'd nearly given up on the whole parenting game. Disappointment had followed disappointment. Serious health complications for his wife had emerged, until finally, they had the privilege of becoming parents. Tess, on the other hand, was of a different generation to Sarge and his wife, and this was likely reflected in her parenting style, not just the modern way her child was presented.

# Tess.

1

Meanwhile, that morning back at Albury Base Hospital, Tess was brought out of the induced coma. The MRI had shown that the swelling in her brain had finally reduced. Her vital signs were promising.

Tess settled back after the flurry of activity when she had come to. A nurse and doctor had patiently sat with her for some time and reacquainted Tess with what they knew of the goings on of this last week of her life, in which she had been, for the most part, unconscious.

A young and kind looking policewoman then called in. Her stated task was to interview the only adult witness the investigation had at its disposal. This took no time at all, because Tess still had no specific memories of anything before packing the eggs and Rachel into her little car on Tuesday, a week ago. It was Tess who really interviewed the constable. She had lots of questions, to fill in the spaces in her mind.

At last, Tess was out of ICU and in a room which had no patient in the bed adjacent to hers. She had a moment to savour the gratitude that she felt in simply being alive with an optimistic prognosis. She soon fell fast asleep again, exhaustion overtaking her. Napping and contemplating was all that she seemed capable of now… that and thankfulness. So thankful was she, that both Rachel and she had been found. She liked the local cop who had located her daughter -in spite of his job title- and Tess rejoiced that he had been at hand for Rachel to trust and come out of hiding. Tess had been reassured again and again that the child was fine, and that Rachel's stay at Desmond House was not forever. The young mum had a huge incentive to get stronger. It puzzled her to learn that Rachel was not talking. This was very out of character for her beloved little chatterbox. However, aside from perhaps a few elusive impressions, Tess frustratingly only remembered things clearly from before the crash. She sipped some more of the ice-cold apple juice and watched the light play through the trees outside her window.

*Hmmm … before the accident, what had been happening?* Tess mused…

Suddenly, Tess sat up straight with a start. Her nearly empty drink fell to the floor. It bounced chaotically instead of shattering, on account of it being plastic and not glass. It came to a stop by the IV trolley. She covered her mouth with her hand. There *was* something she remembered. The strident machine next to her indicated a sudden spike in her blood pressure. A nurse bustled in to check on Tess when the beep of the machine sounded frantically. She frowned at Tess as she scratched out her observations of the chart at the foot of Tess's bed, clucking that she needed to stay calm and rest.

"I just remembered something I need to do at home!" countered Tess in her defence. "If I can call a friend about it, that will help me relax." Tess asked the nurse how to get a direct line out when making a call, without going through the hospital switchboard. When she was by herself again, she made a call with the phone by her bed.

Tess was unaware that this incident was reported to police, as per the instructions left with the Albury Base hospital. The switchboard operator was able to provide the officer following up, with the information that the outgoing call from Tess's room was to a private number. The assigned Albury officer checked her notes and cross-checked her data, underlining her findings: the first call Tess made after regaining consciousness wasn't to a relative, or to Desmond House, or to the social worker who was responsible for Rachel. The young constable could barely suppress her excitement that finally something was happening to relieve her boredom. Babysitting a sleeping witness with amnesia when she did wake, was hardly thrilling.

In the days of Tess's induced coma, the officer had been relegated to the task of putting together the forensic evidence log supplied to Sarge. Ostensibly, she was really a glorified admin support for the tiny Table Top Police Station, with the trickiest unsolved case in its history. The log documented forensic clues like the white paint scraped on the left side of Tess's smashed blue Corolla; Rachel's slipper; the grey army blanket with blood stains; photographs of the blood trails up *Budginigi.* All had been carefully examined, numbered and photographed on the day. It had fallen to her to write it all up, which was not her favourite duty, but it wasn't a long or difficult task.

She wondered how Sarge was going to crack this case, which was scant on clues and witness statements. There was no blood found at the scene that wasn't Tess Moloney's. No helpful size eleven boot-print left on pliable ground. No discarded cigarette, catching-out the offender with their well-known preferred brand. No local priest had been cycling by and seen the accident. No farmer in the field had sighted something unusual and rushed to share it with the police. No perpetrator had given something away over a pint at the pub (yet). This was like no crime episode on television. No witnesses had come forward. The existing witnesses were for all intents and purposes, *incommunicado.* The mother really wanted to remember, but could not, however hard she tried. Hopefully, Sarge was making some sort of progress with the child witness.

2

It became increasingly evident to medical staff, visitors and to Tess herself, that she just wasn't doing well, even though she was making a beautiful physical recovery- apart from some alarming weight loss; the food was terrible at the hospital. Even as a single mother she was able to provide a tastier standard of food at her table. Pancakes with lemon and sugar was what she craved. Rachel would brim with excitement when Tess resorted to this staple favourite when funds were not stretching to the next pension day. She gauged that Rachel never possessed any sense of impoverishment when the treat of pancakes was on the menu. It was a common occurrence but welcomed by Rachel without fail. Tess sighed. She longed to be back in her own kitchen; to sleep in her own bed. When could she be a mother to her child again?

Apart from the bland processed hospital food Tess despised, she assumed that her despondency was a natural result of missing her daughter, and the guilt regarding the upheaval Rachel was experiencing in her little life. Yet there was something more bubbling away under the surface. The staff thought it more psychological than physiological. Tess Moloney seemed dazed and down in the dumps a lot of the time. When she was more like her animated self, she would catch herself out, and lapse into appearing nervous or guilty. She'd decided against phoning Rachel, rightly assessing that if her daughter heard her voice, it might make her more homesick. It would be too difficult to explain to Rachel that she couldn't come home to her just yet. Also, Tess just could not bear facing the reality that Rachel was not talking. It would be too painful and awkward for Tess to keep a one-sided conversation going.

An overworked doctor took a few minutes to sit with Tess on his rounds.

"Don't expect that everything in your life is going to be back to normal too soon. This'll only bring you frustration."

As much as Tess was reassured that amnesia was common with head injuries, she couldn't shake the strangeness, or self-doubt, which seeped into the places not inhabited by sheer relief and the joy of being alive. She battled a palpable sense of loss.

"I lost consciousness and memory. Pictures are missing from the album of my life. How do I know that I haven't irretrievably lost something important? How do I know I will be fit to look after my child? Rachel might be better off in care, then with me. I still feel so dazed. I can't quite intersect with reality. It's like trying to master a tricky jigsaw puzzle with pieces missing, to top it off! I guess I need to know that I've put things back in the right places in my mind before I can take responsibility for someone else."

"Is something else bothering you, Tess? What's this really all about?"

Tess's eyes filled with tears, but she shook her head unconvincing. The regular vivacious Tess who would captivate all with her conversation, who had a laugh which could stop a war, had gone missing. AWOL. She'd brighten a little when mail was brought in with a drawing from Rachel yet suffered not only the separation from her little girl, but from the self-belief, which seemed to have deserted her.

# Sarge

1

At Table Top, after an uncomfortably turbulent flight, Sarge's time in the city seemed surreal. It had been decided that Rachel would remain for at least a couple of weeks in the long-stay program at Desmond House. It was deemed important by Dr Christina King that Rachel learn to trust herself to talk again. Of course, she couldn't go back home until her mother was out of hospital and ready for parenting, anyway.

Sarge had more conventional police work to do than he had engaged with in the previous forty-eight hours. He planned to head into the station, but not before he shared a delightful dinner with his wife and daughter who had sacrificed precious family time for his police duties. *Family first,* Sarge thought ruefully. *Some of the time anyway.*

Anna asked after her playmate with such an earnestness that Sarge was relieved that with all that he couldn't say about Rachel and her situation, he could at least hand over the lovingly drawn picture Rachel had etched for Anna. This brought a radiant smile to his daughter's face and satisfied her concern. She skipped over to the fridge and rearranged the school photos, bills and her own artwork, to place the drawing from Rachel in the centre. Sarge reassessed his intentions to go to the office that evening. One look at his wife's face and he gauged that this wouldn't be at all well received.

*Fair enough too.*

He had spent considerable time with other women and children in the previous couple of days, so he happily helped scrape the dishes from dinner, took the garbage out and watched the late news on the couch, holding his wife's hand. She found him later, lying next to Anna on her bed, storybook resting on his chest, snoozing contentedly. Waking him a little later, they retired together to the master bedroom.

Sarge did the school run the next morning, leaving Sarah free to concentrate on the committee meeting she was to chair that afternoon. Anna pecked him on the cheek and made a beeline for the boisterous game of British Bulldog taking place on the other side of the school yard. She went willingly but without the usual spring in her step. Sarge sighed. He discerned the emptiness too. No Tess driving into the school yard with her tunes blaring. No blonde Moloney kid bobbing around the school steps. He lingered no further and drove to the police station.

The policeman spent a few minutes chatting with Nancy behind the front desk. Finally, arriving at his own desk, Sarge settled back into his ancient office chair. He set his brow with concentration. He had a job to do. Systemically he worked through the intel that Nancy had added from the Albury police. He closed the file, deep in thought.

The overhead fan wobble precariously. The incessant typewriter tapped on and on in the other room as he added his own notebook scrawl to his official report. This staccato symphony drowned out the sound of numerous flies buzzing in their valiant efforts to try to escape their prison between the bent venetian blinds and the window, thick with dust.

Most of the day was spent like this. However, Sarge did make two phone calls. A call was placed to the Manly facility he had only left the day prior. Dr King reported that Rachel had begun the routine of morning lessons at Desmond House. She'd written a book report, worked on subtraction sums and cooked pikelets, all of which was done with confidence and enjoyment.

The school had a custom each day of beginning with a song and the roll marking.

"Great news!" Dr King had reported. The teacher had let Miss Chris know that Rachel's clear soprano was heard singing *Morning has Broken*. The policeman agreed with the psychologist's viewpoint - this was progress and an indicator that Rachel Moloney was getting closer to finding her voice for conversation.

The second call was placed to the region's youth detention centre. After this phone call the policeman stopped to look at the dry paddocks out the window for a long time, deep in thought.

Before he knew it, the clock said school was nearly over and it was time to pick up Anna. He spent five minutes speaking with Mr Holden. Anna sat waiting in the car, she could see the two men speaking and nodding their heads seriously. They shook hands firmly at the conclusion of the conversation. Sarge took Anna home slowly and carefully, listening to her chatter. He repeated much of the routine of the night before, but his mind was elsewhere. It took him ages to fall asleep.

He woke after only dozing off for fifty minutes. The brightness of the moon rising had tricked his body clock into believing it was daybreak. As he lay listening to the regular breathing next to him, he tried in vain to fall back asleep. Instead of focusing on his frustration, he lay there basking in the moonlight and in his good fortune of enjoying his family safe and all together. Years ago, he'd very nearly messed it all up.

He switched his mind back to the present and began ticking off in his mind the file notes he'd added during his day in the office. Yes, he thought with satisfaction, he'd certainly illuminated some important points in the case, and he'd not wasted the hours of wakefulness.

After five hours of sleep, Sarge, dressed in a crisp fresh uniform, snatched a hurried conversation with his family as he drank coffee and coaxed Anna into eating another spoonful of her porridge. After dropping Anna off at school, instead of leaving right away, Sarge parked his police vehicle at the side of the carpark under one of the giant firs. He got out of the car. Breathing deeply the pine freshness, with the crunch of dry nettles underfoot, he smiled. He whistled a radio tune in his distinct baritone, feeling hopeful - he had a lead … or more of a hunch. Observing no activity in the gardens, Sarge ventured out and did a survey of the grounds, finishing with the groundsman's shed. Bob wasn't there and had only been in erratically since Tess's accident.

*Strange. Normally, Bob never misses a day at work.*

Sarge had double-checked the staff sign-in book in the untidy annex of the schoolroom. Just as the principal had indicated when they spoke after school pick-up, the groundsman was at work the day of the accident. There was no chance that Bob had been the one driving the other car. Mr Holden could corroborate that Bob had been on the school site that event-filled day. Sarge too had noticed him on the ride-on mower at the northern end of the school yard. Yet, Mr Holden had also offered that Bob had been away a fair bit since the accident, although he himself did not keep close tabs on the groundsman who was a reliable fixture at the school and who predated himself as an employee there.

"I'm flat out teaching twelve energetic children spanning six grades!" Mr Holden had volunteered emphatically. The sign-in book confirmed that Bob hadn't kept to his regular routine in the days after the hit-and-run and wasn't at work now.

*Why?*

Of course, Bob had been involved in the search for Tess last Wednesday. He may have needed to catch up on some rest, but why had he failed to resume his regular duties?

Sarge checked his notebook as he stood in the shade of the shed. Mr Holden had stated that Bob *had* mumbled something late Thursday when he'd bumped into the principal in the staff kitchenette, about possibly needing some personal leave. Mr Holden had reported that he had a feeling it was family related. Bob had come into the school to turn on some watering systems after the weekend and Mr Holden had thought the old fella looked pale and drawn. In addition to this, Bob seemed to be carrying himself a little gingerly.

*Time to pay Bob a visit, I reckon.* There was only the ants scurrying around, to hear Sarge's resolution spoken out loud.

3

The policeman called into Bob's place on what could have been ostensibly a casual errand, or even a neighbourly visit, given the past hospitality of the lifelong resident of Table Top. Sarge knocked on the door. No one was home. Or so he thought at first. He walked over the ill- kept yard towards the shed. He frowned; this was out of character. Bob was normally very proud not only of the school grounds, but also of his own patch. He was renowned for being testy with kids who he caught littering. Heaven-help any student who was caught interfering with his workshop.

The policeman called *hello* again and headed over to the workshop as it wouldn't be uncommon for Bob to be pottering in the comforting confines of the shed, even if he was feeling a bit under-the-weather.

No dog announced him as he approached. Yes. He'd heard correctly. That was a tractor in operation in a distant paddock.

Calling again, he poked his head around the open shed door. Part of this inviting and immaculate shed housed a modern, well-maintained work bench with a window nearby. Rays of sunshine showed the dance of the dust mites in the spotlight. There was also a section for old farming tools and harvest implements which were carefully suspended on the painted wood wall. Adjacent to this were some hay bales arranged in a sort of yarning circle. Many a mate, and Sarge himself, had shared a beer with Bob there in the cool afternoon breeze on a Sunday arvo. Bob was always happy to interrupt his chores or his tinkering and shoot the breeze with the fellas if they called by.

The policeman was about to withdraw, but his eyes had finally adjusted to the dimness of the other side of the shed - when he noticed a canvas cover shrouding a vehicle.

*Odd,* exhaled the policeman. He hadn't heard that Bob had bought a new car. He called again. No answer. Taking one more step into the gloom, he stood still as his eyes adjusted. He reached out and lifted the corner of the car dust cover. Underneath was no new car, and certainly no collector's item needing special renovations or protection. It was just the same old ordinary ute that Bill used around the place. Ubiquitous utes were a staple of country properties. Sarge deftly examined the front end and bull-bar with his torch. One of the driving lights had taken a hammering and there was unmistakable evidence of a collision. Still, most people around here had 'paddock bashers' on site, (as they are known in Australian idiom). Yet this was the vehicle Bob took to work at Table Top School when he might need the utility to assist with some landscaping of the school grounds. Sarge scratched his chin pensively, he didn't recall noticing that the vehicle showed signs of a bingle, previously. Mr Holden had vouched for his groundsman being at Table Top School when Tess was driving her blue Corolla last Tuesday on route to deliver her eggs. It had been around recess time at the school and the old, yet agile groundsman had been occupied with a ladder in his efforts to remove the football which the pesky Year 6 boys had kicked onto the school house roof. It couldn't have been Bob driving his ute at the time of Tess's accident, but what if someone else had been?

Sarge made his way back to the house and knocked on the old wooden front door. He called out again. He advanced a couple of steps each way on the veranda and was rewarded for his perseverance by the almost imperceptible flick of the curtain.

*Got you.*

Sarge set himself down on the rocking chair, confident that he could win in any battle of wills. He sat rhythmically rocking. So deep was he in his meditation that when the old heeler came from across the paddocks and sniffed his boot, he was startled. He scratched her in between the ears and eventually she settled down at his feet like he was her long-time master.

Sitting companionably, the officer continued his cogitation. The file which Nancy updated daily, stated that another anonymous call had come in while he was in Sydney. The caller claimed that a man with Victorian number plates was seen refuelling a damaged white ute at the lone petrol bowser at the general store. The caller had reported the time as being dusk of the day of the accident.

Ice-creams, fishing tackle and an array of pantry basics could all be bought, along with petrol at the general store. The store was situated close to the weir and the caravan park for the convenience of tourists rather than locals. It was technically plausible that it could have been a tourist who had fled the accident. Sarge concluded that it was far more likely that any offender would head to a service station on the highway with a better chance of anonymity, and continue enroute, away from the scene of the crime. There was nowhere to go from the general store. The Hume weir created a natural boundary, and the driver of the vehicle would need to double back through the hamlet with an obviously damaged car and all the community possibly on alert. It just didn't add up in the policeman's mind. Was this alleged sighting really a convenient way to cast blame away from the town?

Nancy had said that something was off about the call. There was something familiar about the caller's voice, but she just couldn't quite put her finger on it. Besides, the familiar inhabitants of Table Top would ordinarily identify themselves and be up for a chat, or at least exchange pleasantries with the much-loved receptionist. Nancy said that she got the impression that the hasty caller was using a different voice, and their efforts were not completely convincing.

When Sarge had rung the general store yesterday, the owner had disputed that a damaged white ute had been through to purchase petroleum on that evening, as claimed in the anonymous tip-off.

"Mate," he had crackled over the wire. "There was no one matching your description at the petrol pump. There was no one there at all. I was all out of fuel! There was some drama because a pencil pusher further up the food chain couldn't read a blinkin' calendar. The fuel tanker didn't arrive when it was meant to. Petrol wasn't delivered until the day after this supposed sighting. Sarge, your source is not just mistaken, but he's making it up … having you on, mate, that's for sure!" The proprietor chortled with a lack empathy. As much as he respected the local cop, the owner of the general store couldn't help but relish in the absurdity of this "lead" Sarge had received.

The facts at hand seemed to be stacking up. Someone was trying to cast suspicion away from where it was due.

*Feint,* thought Sarge, using a boxing comparison; someone was trying to distract the investigation with a fake punch, to hide the actual blow. A few questions remained, but the policeman felt confident of the picture building in his mind. He had gone over his deductions thoroughly with the evidence at hand. Systematically, Sarge went through his thinking one more time. He started with the first anonymous call. Who would have a gripe enough with the Moloney family and their 'lot' and ring and complain about Tess's ex hanging around, but not want to say it was him complaining?

Then the accident itself was called in. What if that same person had rung again, as the third anonymous caller (with someone acting as his mouthpiece) with the express intention of pointing the investigation in a different direction, what did they hope to gain from this? If they themselves weren't the culprit, then they were surely trying to protect the offender? Why?

Things were becoming clearer. The persons who made the anonymous calls to the station could be one and the same. If the most significant piece of evidence, the vehicle that hit Tess and Rachel, was stored metres away, Sarge could really be making progress in this case, at last!

What would make a cranky but decent bloke, deliberately obstruct an investigation? Surely there were only a few circumstances that would motivate most people to court trouble with the law. Who was Bob covering for?

Sarge looked at his watch, he'd been sitting on the porch for forty minutes. Sitting for a spell on a porch was a country characteristic. He was quite comfortable, but he reckoned with a slight grin that Bob, who was lurking in the house, thinking he could wait out the Sergeant's visit, would be absolutely sweating buckets. The time would have seemed twice as long for him.

"I'm not going anywhere, Bob. You may as well come and face the music," he called out calmly. Sarge waited some more and took out his police notebook in readiness. He carefully wrote the date at the top. Within five minutes at the most, Sarge's strategy was rewarded by the scrape of the front door opening. Bob emerged from the door looking both sick and sheepish.

Sarge nodded but said nothing. In his experience the more nervous someone was, the more readily they would incriminate themselves as they sought to fill in the gaps of silence. Sarge kept rocking gently on the porch like he had no time constraints at all.

Bob looked at the officer uncertainly and eventually sat down on a creaking wooden chair nearby.

After a great many moments had passed, he offered, "Ah, yeah. I'm not feeling great. I don't feel up to having company over. Sorry not to answer the door. Bit silly, really."

Sarge stopped and scrutinised the man. "You look terrible, Bob."

Bob flushed. The policeman did not shift his gaze. Bob squirmed.

"Rotten Flu going round, Sarge. I wouldn't wish it on a mortal enemy."

Sarge's gaze shifted to a nasty cut on Bob's head.

"Top it all off… I had a fall, on account of being dizzy, I expect," explained Bob, noticing the direction of Sarge's gaze.

"See a doctor?"

"Nah, just keeping myself to m'self," Bob slurred.

"Day-drinking won't help you get better, Bob."

"Not against the law, is it?" he retorted. "On my own property! You can't come here and tell me what to do. Come to that, ain't you trespassing on my porch like this?"

"Just being neighbourly, Bob," said Sarge in a soothing tone. "Holden said you haven't been at work regular-like … I thought something might be up. Just checking in on you."

"Holden can mind his own ruddy business," he growled.

Sarge said nothing and began to rock again, biding his time. Bob was sullen. A couple of times he looked as though he might resume talking, but then decided against it. Eventually the sound of the tractor in the paddock stopped.

Out of the corner of his eye, Sarge saw Bob begin to sweat profusely. He felt a little sorry for him, this was certainly tough on the old man.

"It sure is getting warm now, don't suppose you want to get us a cold glass of water?" asked Sarge.

Bob appeared tethered to his chair. Stricken, he couldn't remove himself from witnessing the terrible pantomime unfolding before his eyes.

"Spose, it is about lunch time," Sarge commented as he consulted his watch. He mopped his brow carefully with a clean handkerchief he produced from his pocket. With a loaded casualness he looked directly at Bob and said, "Your boy will be coming in hot and hungry any moment."

At this, Bob jerked up from his chair and it fell over with a crash on the bare boards.

"I know that Jake is home from detention, Bob. Did he borrow your car… is he the driver who hit Tess and Rachel?"

Bob set his chair to rights and slumped down again. He said nothing.

"I've seen the damage to the ute. No need to keep hiding it in your shed now, Bob. Give it up. You can't protect him. Did he give you that touch on the forehead?"

This accusation caused the man to unravel - he'd barely been hanging on by a thread.

"Him hurting me was an accident, Sarge, he just freaked out when I confronted him. He pushed me away and I tripped. The lad would never intend to hurt me."

The sound of tuneless whistling could be heard coming closer.

"Don't warn him, Bob," Sarge cautioned. "It won't go well with you. Already obstructed justice enough. This is serious. Failing to stop at an accident. Negligent driving occasioning bodily harm, driving without a license .... Bob, if Tess had died, God forbid, manslaughter would've been on the table for the lad!"

Bob, looking a waxy grey colour, nodded in submission. They could hear the tap on the side of the house being used as the whistling continued, while presumably the worker washed the dust and grime off his hands. Bad decisions and guilt could never be as easily rinsed off, however.

Jake rounded the house where Sarge and Bob waited. Tall and well-muscled from working out in juvenile detention, he almost looked like an older man, but for the remnants of childhood innocence still detectable in his features.

Taking in the scene, he froze, or more accurately, poised himself to respond. Would he choose fight or flight? Choosing the former, he assumed a studied nonchalance.

"Howdy Sarge," he drawled. "Been awhile." Jake kept his distance. Folding his arms in front of him, he stared back at Sarge.

"Hey Jake. Your Grandad never mentioned you were out early for good behaviour, I had to find out by ringing the warden at Beechworth. I need you to come into the station and answer some questions for me."

"Not sure I need to do that… about what exactly?" Jake spoke with unmistakable attitude. More like a teenager than a man now, but for the depth of his voice.

What a cool customer, thought Sarge grimly. He struggled inwardly for a moment and then opted for the official rhetoric, instead of other phrases that were on the tip of his tongue.

"I've reason to suspect you of being the driver of a vehicle involved in the recent a hit-and-run incident in our community. I need to ask you some questions under caution."

"Are you arresting me, Sarge?" Jake asked with his eyes glittering. "What evidence is there to connect me to that?"

"Look, we need to do this formally. Jake, I've seen the damaged car you have covered in the shed, so it's best if you come in and we do this by the book."

"Hell, Sarge, everyone in town knows that the old man keeps the keys in the ignition. Anyone could've borrowed his ute. You got some evidence I was in it? You got yourself an eyewitness to back up this theory of yours?"

Sarge struggled imperceptibly to keep his temper, and again, won the battle. A vivid picture of Rachel's traumatised face flashed into his mind, when she'd unwittingly communicated that she was threatened not to speak up about what she'd seen. *Settle down* he reasoned with himself. Innocent until proven guilty and all that. Still, he wanted to slap this odious youth up the side of his head. Partly because his gut told him the teenager was an obnoxious liar, partly because technically, the little villain was right.

"I would like you to assist me with my enquiries at the station Jake, let's go. Bob, you need to come too because I need to obtain a statement from you as well."

"Not now," Bob gruffly countered. "On account of me being… ah… a little under the weather."

"Me and the boy will come into the station, first thing in the morning.

Sarge looked from one to the other. He could compromise any evidence given if he insisted that Bob be interviewed officially while intoxicated. Jake overlayed the sneer on his face with a polite, neutral expression. Sarge nodded curtly.

"Fine. I shall look forward to talking with you both, first thing, at the station."

# Rachel

In Manly, Rachel appeared to have adapted easily to her new daily rhythm of lessons in the mornings and free time in the afternoons. She had elected the activity group which allowed her to roam the rocks with the rostered social worker and other kids who'd also chosen this pastime. Once Rachel had been told that her mother was awake and mending well, she was a different child indeed. It was like a fairy had transformed her troubled brow and frail features with a tap of the wand. She seemed content to make the most of the magic of Manly, knowing that she wouldn't be stuck at Desmond House much longer. Her most favourite outing of all was to wander the wonderfully named *Fairy Bower* rock pool, off Marine Parade. It was a charmed place– the sparkling aqua water in the enclosed oblong pool beckoned to those passing by. The bower was virtually a shelf hanging over the endless Pacific Ocean. The water was always lovely and warm, which suited Rachel. In the absence of excess body fat, she would shiver easily, even on a sunny day in the colder water of the open sea.

Rachel roamed the coastline. Sandcastles and sand were overrated in the child's mind. When the wind whipped up she didn't enjoy sand stinging her skin and irritating her eyes. She preferred instead to play amongst the shelter of the many large boulders. She'd gather water-worn stones, constructing towers which were so carefully and delicately balanced.

One day when it was threatening rain, the children brought a snack and sat on the big concrete steps across the road, watching the ocean while munching contentedly. They didn't venture far, walking up and down the paved beach esplanade and climbing a short way up the steps that zig-zagged the cliffs just to the east of Desmond House.

When the promised storm suddenly unleashed its power, they took refuge in a beach pavilion -handy for sheltering from bad weather coming in from ever-changing angles. Rachel loved the time of retreat from the elements as much as the perfect sunny afternoon previous, poking anemones and crabs and splashing in the rock pools. Rachel liked that the beach shelters were painted the colour of potato chips. She admired their lovely large white arched windows. Inspired by *Play School*, the kids asked their leader to transport them through the arches and tell them a story, while they huddled together, waiting for the storm to settle. They were told the true tale of a clever sand sculptor, who'd displayed his life-sized sand sculptures of people and scenes in one of the larger Manly beach pavilions. This helped to prolong the life of his creations, rather than making them on the beach. The amazing artist would tint his pieces with a colour wash to make them more realistic. So clever.

One of Rachel's many grievances with playing with sand was the frustration of building a castle or fort on the beach only to see it fall because of the tide or wind. That is of course, if some other kid didn't jump on her castle first.

In class, capitalising on the fascination of the children with the sculptor, the teacher devoted some time in morning lessons for them to learn more about John Suchomlin, who displayed his work in this neighbourhood in the late 1920s to the early 1930s. The children were shown glossy photographs of his depictions of the Nativity, Easter and Anzac scenes. Rachel was fascinated with Suchomlin's adventurous life. She was mesmerised by his story of escaping Russian unrest by becoming a stowaway on multiple ships. The Ukrainian immigrant who became an Australian citizen, was extraordinary. His work rivalled Madame Tussaud's wax works, but the only lasting evidence of his sculptures made of sand and water were the photographic postcards he sold, or news clippings. Rachel's favourite settings were those with mermaids in them. She also looked for a long time at the photograph of *Soul's Awakening,* where the rapt face of a sand-sculpted young woman made an impression on her.

Rachel was genuinely enjoying the days at Desmond House, even though Sarge and Liza had left. It was truly a wonderful program for country kids, giving them treatment or therapy they couldn't access in rural Australia. Lessons were tailored to individual learners in the mornings with kids having a wonderful time in the city or at the beach, in afternoons.

Rachel still didn't like the food, but she did appreciate the fun atmosphere in the dining room, which made her feel like she was on a camp every single day. Most of the staff which included nurses, doctors, social workers, teachers and even the cook (who would dart out of the kitchen to joke with the kids and dare them to have second helpings)- showed genuine commitment and care for their charges.

When Rachel was admitted to the long stay program, she'd left the comfortable room she'd shared with Liza to move into the dormitories, which were essentially hospital wards. After all, Desmond House was a medical institution and couldn't completely disguise this. The boys were segregated in a different building from the girls. Rachel had her own cubicle in the girl's wing, but none of the children ever utilised their curtains. Her hospital locker kept the few personal possessions she'd brought with her. Every day the children would choose a taped bundle of clothes from a room near the communal bathroom. Rachel enjoyed the lucky dip of what she'd dress herself in each day.

The novelty of all this didn't always serve as a distraction, however, for the long nights she experienced in the ward. She, along with all the others, slept in high and narrow hospital beds. On the second night, rolling over in a restless dream, she tumbled out of bed, waking in surprise, sore on the floor. Most of the time though, she couldn't sleep, for thinking. Fraught with worry, she felt like a rubber band which was taut and ready to *whizz* across the room once released, or snap.

Really sick kids, or those recovering from operations, were kept in the upstairs ward where the nurse's station faced the sleeping children. The remainder of the children were largely those referred to Desmond House for issues which were social, behavioural or psychological, with minor medical concerns. Many children were referred to the facility to access help because they lived in remote places, but others were just in bad home situations. The long-stay program sometimes functioned as a waiting room for kids who'd be shunted into permanent care if their home situations couldn't be made safer.

In the general wards, the night-duty nurse slept in a small room down the hall. This meant that the oldest, bossiest, meanest, most troubled girl, often had the opportunity to tyrannise her dorm. Random acts of violence could never be entirely ruled out.

On her second night, Rachel was dragged out of her bed unceremoniously and thrown down the stairwell. Fortunately, she somehow rolled and landed on her feet with the agility of a cat, and no real harm was done. Unbeknownst to her, silent Rachel had offended an aggressive older girl, shortly after her admission to the wards.

"Speak up!" A girl with greasy hair and glittering eyes had growled at her when she'd passed her on the way to the shower room.

Perhaps, her bully took umbrage at Rachel's lack of compliance in supplying conversation, or maybe the older girl was accustomed to targeting any new girl.

When Rachel fell victim to this thuggery, her legs somehow remained wrapped in one of her stiff cotton sheets for part of her journey from bed to stairs. After Rachel had collected herself, she listened to gauge if her persecutor and moved on, and then she scampered up the stairs and retrieved the sheet. She wrapped herself up tightly in the cotton and slept on the landing for a few hours until she deemed it safe to creep back to what had become most inhospitable sleeping quarters. The next morning, she wondered if she'd dreamt it all. Her bruises and the scuffed sheet, torn at an edge, told her it was not just a nightmare. She carefully tucked the evidence away when she made her bed adeptly and put everything in good order. All the children as part of the discipline of the institution were taught to make their beds immaculately, complete with hospital corners. Matron inspected all the wards before the children were released to go down for breakfast at 7:30am.

Instinctively, she decided to say nothing of what had happened, for fear of reprisals. Fortunately for Rachel, her bully exited the centre the next day, but it did demonstrate that all the good work done in the day with the children could be undone at night. Ever resilient, Rachel seemed to cope with the nights away from home and embrace the days with gusto.

# Sarge

Sarge didn't sleep much the night after his visit to Bob and Jake's place yet was fresh and prepared for their arrival the next morning. Bob and Jake attended the station promptly at nine o'clock, however the attitude of both grandfather and grandson made the policeman wonder if scheduling the interview might have been for nothing.

Bob went first and made it clear that he was speaking with Sarge voluntarily. The interview quickly took a dismal yet comedic turn, with Bob backing up Jake's reasoning of the day prior. Bob claimed that he only *suspected* that Jake had borrowed his car, he didn't know it. He, like the police, had no proof, he insisted.

Bob agreed that he'd come out of school that fateful Tuesday to discover that his ute was not in the school car park. He said he wasn't too concerned at first, thinking that the young fella - not long home- had got jack of farm work and walked the quarter mile that stood between home and Table Top school, to grab the vehicle. Bob acknowledged that it looked bad for Jake. He'd been sentenced to a stint of juvenile detention because he was caught at the age of fifteen, driving drunk, on one of the few sealed roads in their area. No licence of course. Most kids did it. Most kids like Jake could drive better than many older citizens, even before they were of age to obtain a licence.

So yes, Bob conceded, it wouldn't have done for Jake to admit he'd been in the driver's seat of the ute, with only his learner plates, and when he'd not yet completed the driver safety course, which was mandatory for young offenders.

Bob was adamant however, that despite his fears, when he got home the car was not there, and Jake was mucking out the chicken coop. Bob said that he immediately assumed that he'd been stupidly forgetful and had left his vehicle up at the top of the school hill at the side access road where he had hauled some gear earlier in the day. Ruefully he admitted it wasn't the first time that he'd forgotten that he'd parked there. Unconcerned, he'd cooked his steak and eggs for lunch, before heading back to the school.

Jake had declined his offer to join him for lunch, teasing his grandad that he would give himself a coronary or obesity if he lunched like that every day. Bob recounted how he took his time and had a second cup of black tea while he read the paper. He liked to keep out of the sun for a spell. He walked the short distance back to school after his leisurely lunch hour, arriving at 1:30pm, like normal. He'd chuckled to himself when he spotted his vehicle at a distance on the northern perimeter of the school. He really thought he was going daft in his old age.

It was when he was passing the school room that Mr Holden dashed out to tell him that Tess Moloney's vehicle had been found crashed on Mitchell Road but was mysteriously empty. The principal had told Bob that there was no sign of the mother, or her charge, who was sick and in her care. Town folks were putting together a search team. It was assumed that Bob would join, and the principal released him from his school duties. There was no need for Bob to take his own car as a fellow RFS volunteer would come by the school to collect Bob in the truck. Bob insisted that it was dark when he was finally dropped back to the school to fetch his ute (as Sarge would well know, because it was, he who'd found the poor little lass at sunset). Bob claimed that because he'd driven it home in the dark, it was only the next morning that he'd noticed the damage.

Bob admitted that it was at this stage that he'd become frantic. He wondered if Jake might've overplayed the joking and conversation at lunch. He'd leaped to the conclusion that Jake had borrowed the car to visit a mate or something and had crashed and then returned the vehicle.

"Sarge, I jumped the gun… just like you are. Someone else could have borrowed the car. Where's your proof that it was the lad? Look I did the wrong thing, I know. I panicked at the thought that it was my ute used in the hit-and-run and tucked it away in the shed. I admit, my mind did go straight to Jake being behind the wheel. Saddens me to think that I did. I'd hoped that all that trouble was behind him. Jake's a good boy at heart. Jus' went off the rails since his mum succumbed to cancer. Pretty rough for him to lose her when he was only thirteen and have to come and live with his granddad."

"So yes… I'm guilty of wanting to cover it up! My first instinct was to protect him, just in case. Don't tell me you wouldn't instinctively take that stance for your kin… well, if you weren't no copper. No disrespect intended, Sarge. My statement will stand. There's no proof that Jake did it, whatever his fool grandfather thought or did!"

At this the old timer set his jaw and would say nothing more.

Nancy, working overtime with the extra activity at the station, couldn't resist giving the taciturn interviewee a cup of tea and a bulging homemade sandwich when it was Jake's turn to be interviewed. She remembered his late wife and daughter well and had considerable compassion for Bob and his situation.

*Round Two*, thought Sarge ruefully. In the interview room just metres away from where Bob was munching on his sandwich, Jake was sticking to his story. He claimed he was at home working on the farm on the Tuesday when the accident occurred.

"Can anyone verify that?"

"What, like an alibi? Jake scoffed sarcastically. "Yeah right! Loads of people were queuing up to do manual labour on our patch of land. Of course no one was helping me chip burrs on the property! The way I see it, no one can say I wasn't."

*And no one had so far,* thought Sarge. No one had *said* anything. Sarge tried to draw Jake out from his defensive position. "What are your long-term plans, now you have done your stint in *juvie*, Jake?"

"Dunno really, 'spose I'll stick around and help Grandad for a bit. I hate this backwater though! What a fishbowl! Everyone watching everybody else's business. Costs me nuffin' though, 'til I work out what's next."

"You've filled out since I last laid eyes on you, lad. You look really fit and well, Jake. I guess that's one good thing from your time away."

Jake grunted, non-committal, but he didn't disagree.

Sarge didn't try to fill the gap. He just waited.

"Yeah, well, I did a lot of exercise when we were locked into our cells for the night. Kept me from freaking out," he said with a hint of accusation.

"For what it's worth mate, I would have recommended probation and community service. The magistrate was likely concerned about the gang you were running with. Stealing the car for a joy ride no doubt tipped the court to give you a custodial sentence, even as a youth."

Jake wouldn't make eye contact for several minutes.

"Guess I was angry and stupid after mum died," he said flatly. "The thing is though, *juvie* is pretty much a gang scene anyway, so the justice system isn't real smart either."

Toning down the belligerence, Jake offered, "I did do a fair bit of sparring while I was in there. Helped me with the boredom... and I really liked the strategy - gave me something to think about, so I didn't go bonkers. Yeah, both the fitness and mind work appealed to me."

"Yep. I thought the same when I got into boxing at the Police Boys Club when I was a teen. I was light on my feet and well-muscled, in those days." The sergeant stated this factually, without self- deprecation.

Jake relaxed visibly.

"You been keeping up with Ali's upcoming fight at the New Orleans Super Dome, Sarge? Ali's been getting back into shape to defend his 10th title."

"'Course, I'm a huge fan. Did I see some ink, in honour of the great man himself?"

Sarge was confident that he'd made out enough details of the tell-tale tattoo. Yesterday, Jake had been dressed in a singlet, with his work shirt tied around his waist, when he'd emerged from the side of the house.

"Yeah. My last hurrah before my freedom was taken from me."

Jake unbuttoned his long-sleeved shirt there in the interview room. He slipped his arm out, proudly displaying an angry-faced bee morphing into a resplendent butterfly. Both gained the appearance of movement when Jake flexed his bulging bicep.

Sarge whistled appreciatively and mouthed the inscription weaved through the design in modified cursive, "Float like a butterfly. Sting like a bee."

Slipping his shirt back over his shoulder, Jake grinned at the police officer in front of him and looked at Sarge pointedly, "Never too late for you to get fit again Sarge."

Sarge chuckled but carefully changed tack. "Man's gotta know when he's on the ropes, Jake." He paused to let that sink in to his opponent. "I'd like to direct your attention to document 16A."

Sarge slipped a quality photocopy from the file under his arm. He turned over Rachel Moloney's drawing and slid it across the table to Jake, rapping his knuckles on the scarred wooden table of the interview room.

Jake's smile faded into a grimace. His eyes changed like shutters, coming down in just one blink.

"What's this meant to be?" Jake growled, his attitude back.

"Son, this here is evidence from eight-year-old Rachel Moloney who's the *child* victim of the hit-and-run we're questioning you about. She's been too traumatised to speak since, but with the support of a court-appointed psychologist, she was able to draw this picture to communicate what she remembered of the car accident - and of the driver who bailed after frightening the life out of her."

Sarge took a long pause and let Jake squirm in his seat.

"Look… you weren't completely heartless; it was you who put a blanket over little Rachel's unconscious mother, Tess. You did call it in… right?"

Jake said nothing.

"The thing is, not only can we connect you to the crime scene now, but we're gonna get you and grandad on obstruction too. You and he made an 'anonymous' call, trying to direct police attention elsewhere. That'll play well in court," Sarge stated with heavy sarcasm.

Jake shook his head mechanically - whether from denial or disbelief that the interview had galloped in a dangerous direction.

Sarge continued, making the switch from *good cop* to *bad cop*. "If this were boxing, Jake, we could say that making that call was a *feint*. But none of this is just sport, is it Jake? So, we've added obstruction of justice to your rap sheet. What else? You're facing a stack of charges mate… driving without a licence, breaking your parole conditions, negligent driving, leaving the scene of an accident, intimidating a witness. You're in very serious trouble. As we speak, the ute is being impounded by NSW Police for forensic examination."

Sarge paused his delivery, to determine if it'd hit its mark.

Jake's face showed shock. *Yes! Got you!* Some of his evidence was circumstantial, but bang-on, he reckoned. *Bless Christine and her expertise.* Without the drawing, he would have nothing to frighten Jake into seeing that his anonymity was over.

The heavy pause lingered. No man's land lay between him and the young offender. Sarge willed himself not to show his nervousness. He knew his case mightn't have sufficient evidence to hold up in court without a confession.

Jake had made an error of judgement, undoubtedly, when he'd chosen to drive unlicensed. He'd believed the lie that he was impervious to the law in the tiny town of Table Top (even though his previous conviction said otherwise). It'd all gone horribly wrong for Jake when he'd failed to give way, driving around the country lanes like he owned them. He was at fault… but maybe not for the mess that Tess had made of herself by failing to wear a seat belt. Still, leaving her there like that wasn't his finest moment, even if his actions were not borne from malice, but from desperation. He could never have foreseen the double calamity: first, Rachel running off and then, of all things, Tess coming to and wandering off, disoriented and searching for her daughter, only to sustain further life-threatening injuries. Jake was barely an adult himself, and no doubt he'd said something dumb to panic the child enough for her to flee. Damaging words, with power over the child witness still.

Randomly, he reflected that Miss Chris would agree with his assessment - the young offender had displayed classic fight and flight responses. What a nightmare he had created.

Sarge didn't trust himself to not say or do something ridiculous, if he waited any longer. "Well, it's time to come clean Jake, what do you have to say for yourself? Will you help us bring this case to a close for the sake of a mother and child who've suffered enough?"

Jake had no bravado left; the fight was gone. He knew plenty firsthand about the suffering of a mother and child. He'd shocked himself at how the whole situation had escalated.

"Orright, I'll give you what you want, but I want you in return to forget my grandad as an accessory after-the-fact... if I put my hand up for this. Deal? I want a solicitor present."

The policeman nodded his consent. "Smartest move yet, lad."

# Rachel

As the days went by while Jake awaited his court hearing and faced the likelihood of further detention, Tess convalesced in Albury Hospital and Rachel stayed on at Desmond House. Tess and Rachel had brightened considerably, once it became clear that they would indeed be reunited soon. They each had the motivation to get well. Mother and daughter tolerated institutional life as a temporary but essential measure. There were numerous personal kindnesses from staff and the community, which helped restore their fragile trust in humanity.

Rachel put on a little beneficial weight and epitomised a bronzed Aussie with her tanned limbs and sun-bleached, sea-washed hair. Not surprisingly, she seemed freer since she was informed of Jake's cooperation. Though, why she'd kept his identity under wraps still needed to be determined. There was possibly another layer to this complicated story. When Sarge had brought Anna for a day visit one weekend, it was like a load had lifted from Rachel's diminutive shoulders. Sarge was very pleased but remained relentless in his commitment to tie up all the loose ends of this case, and to play his part in putting fractured lives back together, where he could.

Rachel, still not speaking, was not completely silent either. She laughed easily these days. She could be heard singing with gusto, often enough, in school time, or crooning softly to herself as she played on the rocks and collected shells. Not yet talking, she'd instead become increasingly expressive and adept at non-verbal cues. She'd lost the habit of speech.

With the arrival of Anna for a visit, the staff (and Sarge) had hoped that with all that there was to catch up on, Rachel's tongue would be loosened. But it wasn't so. Anna chattered away and Rachel listened with a delighted smile. She shrugged her shoulders, nodded or shook her head as was required. She didn't chatter back. However, Rachel was clearly elated to be with her friend for the day and content with the promise that she'd be back at Table Top school sooner rather than later. There was a shared understanding between the two girls on a range of matters which rendered speech redundant. The psychologist grasped this but remained puzzled by what was holding Rachel back. There was still a blockage to Rachel fully processing and moving on from the trauma of whatever had transpired in the aftermath of the car crash.

In their sessions, Miss Chris consistently referenced the fact that the young man who'd crashed into her mother's car had been caught by clever Sarge. Jake had admitted his fault. Yet even though Rachel had initially expressed excitement and real pleasure at this development, she'd suddenly and quickly drawn the curtain on her reaction.

# Sarge and Tess

Sarge took matters into his own hands. After an off-the-record chat with Jake, he extrapolated the information he needed and went to visit Tess in hospital for a quiet conversation. He made it clear that he was coming as a neighbour and not as the law. Holding Tess's hand, he assured her that the community was still arranging for her chickens and gardens to be cared for. Lambsie was staying at Foster's farm. He told her of some of Rachel's adventures in Sydney. This was like a tonic for the young mum's frayed nerves.

Before he left her hospital room the officer aimed some carefully chosen words at his target. With minimal fuss, Sarge kindly indicated to Tess that he'd taken the liberty of removing the *junk,* (as he phrased it, whilst clearing his throat gruffly) which had been building up in the shed at her place.

*She needn't concern herself with sorting out that mess. They need never talk about it again.*

Tess's eyes had widened, and her face paled at this news. Then there were tears and thanks expressed, then a lovely smile which began as a brightness in her eyes.

From that point on, the progress Tess made in her recovery increased exponentially. Another layer of complexity and trouble fell away.

Sarge had discreetly dealt with the situation that he'd suspected ever since the report of Tess's reactions after she awoke from the induced coma. No wonder Tess had seemed close to panic when she visualised police and neighbours pottering around her property, with a shed crammed with the spoils of criminal activity. Tess had unwisely agreed to house some stolen merchandise for a friend of a friend, with the lure of some extra cash. Jake had explained how he'd overlapped with some of the same gang of petty criminals, who Tess's boyfriend had a previous connection to. Jake had discovered that it was Tess who was storing the stolen goods. This was the source of the threat that Jake had made to Rachel, when he had roughly whispered into her ear, "There are stolen things in your shed. I know all about 'em. Your mummy will go to jail if I tell on her. She will be taken away from you! I won't tell on her, if you don't tell on me. It's our secret. Got it? Don't tell!"

A powerful pledge to place a child under.

# Rachel

The greatly desired breakthrough came on a second weekend trip to Manly, when Sarge and Anna visited Rachel again. They'd enjoyed a wonderful morning which included a ferry ride and fish and chips by the beach.

Anna sat with some books in the courtyard, and Sarge joined Miss Chris for a session with Rachel. Seated on a bright rug on the floor, they'd cooperatively built a huge tower and city with blocks.

They chatted with the little witness as they played together. Sarge told the child that Jake had admitted that he'd threatened her and sworn her to secrecy, but Rachel needn't worry about that anymore.

"Mum isn't going to get into any trouble. Jake made a mistake. The stuff in your shed is gone. Jake wants to tell you that he is very, very sorry for frightening you, Rachel."

Sarge considered for a moment all the harm that had quickly escalated after the collision. As they built with the blocks, he breathed a sigh of gratitude. Things were finally being put to rights. The stuff in the shed had been removed and returned to their owner, by a third-party Sarge had arranged. He was confident that he'd enough connections to keep the matter quiet. Rachel had nothing to fear coming home. She didn't need to protect her mother any longer. There was no reason for her to stay silent.

Miss Chris assured Rachel, "Grown-ups should never make children promise not to talk."

Rachel sat still, absorbing all this information which was gently communicated to her. A crease on her forehead evaporated. Suddenly, Rachel pushed over the tower they'd been building with one sweep of her arm. She giggled at the mess and clatter she had made. Miss Chris and Sarge scooted back from the sudden ruckus, chuckling. Clambering up, Rachel hugged each of the adults in turn. Looking down on Miss Chris's gleaming ponytail and Sarge's receding hairline, she then kissed them each gently on the tops of their heads.

Running into the foyer, she called out to Anna, "Quick, come on, Anna! I want to tell you all about my favourite places here!"

# Epilogue

A slightly more mature looking Tess Moloney made her way into the crammed school hall just before the house lights were dimmed. Hair soft and shiny, eyes dancing, she made self-deprecating jokes out of the corner of her mouth to Sarge who was sitting beside her. Tess was looking well. She'd blossomed into a beautiful young woman. She'd nearly left behind the stigma of teenage pregnancy, and even if she'd never completely shake the feeling that she was a fraud, she could at least live with it.

She didn't love school events, but here she was making a rare appearance as a doting school mum, for the sake of her daughter. It'd been a rush to make it on time, and if Sarge had not saved her a seat, she would've had to resort to lurking in the back corner, which did hold appeal for her.

Tess vainly craned her neck looking for Rachel in the dark. She could be sitting with Grade Four, or maybe she'd already be backstage, excitedly waiting for her class's turn to take the stage for the end of year performance night.

The Moloney's never rejoined community life at Table Top. Tess deemed a fresh start was necessary and had severed almost all lingering entanglements. The dream of building a hobby farm in a small village was gone. Tess didn't want to live under scrutiny. She and her child had received too much attention already. She'd exchanged the poultry and paddocks for an Albury townhouse with a small, easy-maintenance yard. There was room only for a trampoline and fernery in the backyard. No more chickens, just a tamed magpie for a pet that they fed with minced meat daily.

Liza had suggested staying at Table Top, thinking that the stability of the same school would be better for Rachel. Tess had disagreed with the social worker whose role was to advise and support, rather than dictate. It was Tess's prerogative to reinvent herself and what better time than when they were finally reunited as a little family, to start afresh. So much had already disrupted their life at Table Top. Tess followed her instincts and started Rachel at a new school, her third school in her short educational career. Rachel, ever resilient, settled in well, even though she arrived in the middle of a school term. She embraced the opportunity to start again.

Sarge of course was no longer able to cast a daily protective eye on the family, as his beat remained at Table Top. Indisputably, he'd played an important part in the lives of the Moloney mother and daughter, and he contented himself with that. Each week he would drive the twenty minutes into town so Anna could attend a dancing lesson with Rachel. Not Sarah, though. Ostensibly, she'd gone to look after her aged parent in the city. Sarge wondered if she would return to Table Top at all. Would he have to make a choice, and leave Table Top to keep his wife? Would she even want that?

Sarge would often treat the girls to a milkshake together after ballet. They got along better than sisters since they didn't live in each other's pockets, but they considered each other as kin of sorts. Sarge felt privileged to have not just done his duty, but to have been a positive force in a family who were on the knife's edge of self-destruction. He knew a couple of the teachers at Rachel's new school and was satisfied that her new *village* would support Tess in the raising of Rachel. This new community accommodated, encouraged and even prayed for both Tess and Rachel. Sarge welcomed reports of how Rachel thrived. She'd found her voice, yet at the same time she possessed a canny ability to camouflage herself against the new terrain. While not always conforming to school systems, Rachel needed and loved the school routine. For a child who'd been exposed to way too much unpredictability in her small world, school was safe and dependable. Most of the teachers gave her the right amount of rope- knowing when to relax their grip, and when to tighten.

Tess and Sarge sat up straighter when Rachel stepped in front of the curtain and introduced the opening performance of the night. Her class would present an original item written by their teacher. Gone was the silent, cagey child. Rachel confidently enunciated her lines, barely glancing at her script. 4C had been exploring different occupations in class and this item would showcase how the future held so much possibility for each of them. Rachel's voice rang out clearly, with just the right amount of cadence needed to capture the attention of the crowd.

"Please enjoy all of tonight's items!"

The audience smiled encouragingly. Parents were happy the presentations had finally started, so they could get to the part quicker where they'd take their kid's home to bed and settle themselves in for a bit of telly for the evening. Rachel scuttled away to take her place with the others.

The curtains opened to reveal a scene reminiscent of an American pageant where the children were decked out with brightly coloured cardboard sandwich-boards. The children had painted these themselves in the shape of symbols of various occupations. Their teacher had drawn most of the shapes and used a box cutter to cut out the designs.

Titters of amusement sprang up from the audience as the students, grinning proudly, shuffled forward to synchronise their steps, bumping each other into the formation of a horseshoe. One-by one, each student stepped forward and sang a verse about what they wanted to be when they grew up. As each student stepped back, the rest of the class would sing back the verse. Child after child had their moment in the spotlight, and the audience genuinely enjoyed each delightful presentation.

Tess readied herself with the camera as her own child stepped forward. Sarge's heart swelled as he witnessed his little witness take her place. Rachel's career had been carefully matched to her, even though her other classmates had to draw their occupation out of a hat. Yet, all her classmates recognised the rightness of Rachel's assigned career, they didn't begrudge her this small show of favouritism.

Rachel took a deep breath, with eyes bright and her heart-shaped chin tilted slightly, she sang out sweetly, melodiously even:

*An author, an author, I want to be an author*

*With tales of hope and mystery*

*I'll torture and delight!*

As she stepped back to join the curve of her peers, even the audience joined in the refrain:

*An author, an author, she wants to be an author*

*With tales of hope and mystery*

*She'll torture and delight!*

# Thanks

Brian Purcell: Editing

Natalie Petrohelos: Proof reading

Graham Davidson: Cover design

M Leigh Photography: Author photo

Day Media

Wickham Writers (Hunter Writers Centre)

NVCS' first Secondary students and pilot readers of *Child Witness.*

Rod Ritchie, Connor & Sarah, Ella & Ashlyn

# About the Author

Renee Ritchie is a writer of Literary Fiction. She enjoys aspects of both country and coast life, dividing her time between the two locations of Narrabri and Newcastle, New South Wales. She is an Ordained Minister (ACC) and currently teaches English and French to teenagers.

www.ingramcontent.com/pod-product-compliance
Lightning Source LLC
Chambersburg PA
CBHW040530170726
48295CB00012B/410